# I am the Lord
## Second Edition

## By

## Ezhuth Aani

**Myth Publications**

Jamaica

New York

United States of America

# *Dedication*

*To those who taught me*

Ezhuth Aani

# About the Author

The author is a medical practitioner in the USA. He has published an anthology of poems, and two novels Enthaiyum Naane (2014), Angaharam (2015) in Tamil. In addition, he has published Another Tale of Two Cities (2016, 2022), bRAINBOW (2016), Riding with Ravan (2021, 2022), and Painted Surgeon (2021) in English. He has published many short stories, poems, and articles in Tamil and English. This is the second edition of his debut novel in English.

Born in Jaffna, Sri Lanka, the author has seen the ravages of the civil war in that country. He has lived and worked as a medical doctor in five countries in four continents. He has worked with or treated people from over 100 countries. Drawing from his unique life experiences, his writings reflect an international perspective.

Cover design: Steven Lev MD

I am the Lord

# Contents

Ezhuth Aani

# Myword

Religion is an emotive issue and religious strife is one of the main causes of war in the modern world.

Religion is something with which we are born. We cannot change our natural parents. Nor can we change the colour of our skin. Similarly, religion too cannot be changed. So I thought. During my childhood, I had friends from many different religions. We never thought those from a different religion are different to us. But, when I travelled to the Western countries, I saw for the first time proselytizing, religious conversion, mind control and other ugly sides of religion. I also saw that some people made a career out of religion and that their happiness and economic prosperity depend on converting other people to their way of thinking.

The arguments and counter arguments that arose when friends tried to convert me form the underlying philosophy of this story. I have tried to walk a tight rope between making my point with clarity and hurting others' sentiments. In spite of my best intentions, if I have hurt anyone, I apologise profusely.

I am proud to say that I have read the Bible from cover to cover at the request of my friends. The more I delved into it, the more I realised that religion forms the basis of our cultural identity. No

I am the Lord

religion or culture is superior or inferior to another. When one changes religion, ones roots are severed. We come under the control of others. When one of the spouses converts, it places unnecessary stresses on the family.

A society that places so much emphasis on freedom of choice and informed consent observes a deafening silence when those who are terminally ill, who are invalid or even those who have lost their mind are converted under direct or indirect duress. What hypocrisy is this?

Religion has nothing to do with spirituality. Those who do not respect others' religions cannot be spiritually mature. When a bad person does bad things, we can explain it by their nature. When a good person does bad things, such as commits a murder, surely religious or political brainwashing is involved.

When we place our identity and independence in the hands of others, we lose control over our lives. This is what those who seek to peddle religious cults for their own benefit want.

Usually people have filters in their brain that remove any input that is a threat to one's independence. However, by various psychological tactics, these defences can be bypassed or overcome and certain ideas can be planted in the innermost realms of one's thought process. It is much easier to achieve this when someone is under emotional stress due to some reason. The tactics include but are not limited to scare mongering (example: end of world prophecies), financial incentives and seemingly logical arguments that are based on internal verification only (for example proving that a certain prophecy came true, based on a subsequent chapter of the same source as the original prophecy). Once the idea is planted, the Gurus can get the disciple to do almost anything they want.

I cannot but compare the religious guru-disciple relationship to a BDSM Dominant – Submissive relationship. Many intelligent highfliers get caught up in this because relinquishing power to the Guru can help them relax away from their busy and stressful careers. This is akin to a submissive giving up control in BDSM. However, if the Dominant has a hidden agenda, this can result in a disaster. Apart from the obvious economic exploitation, cultural and political invasions could be facilitated through this mechanism. This is very relevant to countries such as India.

When this novel was originally published in Tamil, it had a good reception and many eminent people requested that this be translated into English. I would like to express my sincere thanks to Prof Parvati Vasudev who helped me with the translation. I would also like to acknowledge my publisher in Tamil, the late Espo, a great writer himself, who encouraged me to write my debut novel. And certainly Dr. Parvathi Nagasundaram, my aunt, who laid the foundation for my English at an early age. Last but least my sincere thanks to my wife Dr. Mythily Ramanathan for supporting me through the good times and bad in life. I wish to thank Steven Lev MD who kindly created the cover design.

If by reading this book at least one person is able to get out of religious mind control and starts to think clearly, my mission would be deemed fulfilled.

Ezhuth Aani
(Anantha Ramanathan)
May 2022

# PART I

# PAIN

I am the Lord

# 1

As soon as he landed in Tamilnadu, he felt like prostrating and worshipping the ground. He was proud that his feet were on the sacred land that had enjoyed the prosperity and glory of the reigns of the Chera, Chola, Pandiya, and Pallava kings. At the same time, he wondered, with a feeling of inferiority, whether he was worthy of this honour.

Yes. Though he grew up in Australia, he had read and immersed himself in the writings of the famous historical novelists of the bygone era, such as Sandilyan and Kalki Krishnamurthy.

When he went to Australia, he was ten. The events of the '83 riots, when his house was burnt, his belongings looted, and how as refugees his family had sought asylum in Australia, were as deeply etched in his memory, as if they had all happened the day before. How they had left their house with the clothes they were clad in, how in fear and nervousness, they had huddled together in the hut behind their house, and then gone to the refugee camp, and finally, how they had landed in Australia — all these events had left an indelible mark on his mind.

A problem-free, peaceful life for eight years ensued. Now he had come in search of his roots.

Ezhuth Aani

His father had arranged this trip in celebration of his having gained admission into a medical college.

With his Australian passport, visa, and other documents were cleared at the immigration counter without any hassles. He arrived at the luggage section as one of the first ten passengers. He had to wait for a while, until his baggage came to him swaying on the conveyor.

It was common for those who finished their immigration formalities early to leave the airport last, and for those who completed their immigration formalities late to leave the airport early. This is the law of life. It was common knowledge that, first rankers in school often changed track later in life, while mediocre teenagers often became achievers later in life. We know of several scientists and political leaders who have blossomed late. The rat race of life is not a 100 metres run. It is a marathon. One may be offered numerous opportunities all through life to progress. Those who seize them persistently, achieve the final victory in life.

With these thoughts, he observed the luggage items that passed in a queue on the conveyor. He reflected on how people identified their own baggage. When we meet our relatives, we do not recognize them by their height, weight, or characteristics. On the contrary, we recognize our acquaintances the moment we see them. Can we identify our travel bags, which we use once in a way, thus? We have to recollect their colour, size,

I am the Lord

lock, seal, and so on, before recognizing our own bags. This being so, he wondered how difficult it should be for the police to nab 'unknown' criminals, based only on the evidence provided by several witnesses.

As his thoughts wandered in this manner, a particular big, beautiful suitcase caught his attention. He wondered what prevented a stranger from walking away with such items of luggage. On one hand, they might contain valuables. On the other, there might be prohibited substances such as drugs, in them. While handling others' possessions, we may incur either good or bad; that is the law of life.

He was jolted from his philosophical reflections, by the arrival of his suitcases. Brushing aside his flights of imagination, he paid attention to his clearing the Customs' formalities.

By the time he left the airport, engaged a taxi, and sat back, he felt tired. The moment Sivan, the taxi driver, realized that the passenger had come from abroad he raised his fare manifold. Though he knew that he was being exploited, he did not wish to register his disapproval by engaging another taxi. He knew that all taxi drivers were alike. He knew he was being over charged but he wanted to reach his father's friend's house in T'Nagar, safely and as soon as possible. So, he paid the fare that was demanded, and got in.

Ezhuth Aani

# 2

The woman waiting at the door asked him, "Come in my boy, how's your father? My husband has gone out on some work. He'll be back soon."

His name was Jagan. He was ten years old, when the '83 riots occurred. Their family lived in the suburbs of Colombo. He was studying at the Royal College, where the children of the elite were being educated. His sister was studying in St. Bridget's Convent, one of the leading women's colleges. His father, Mr Nagaraja, was an accountant in a hospital in Colombo. His mother was a teacher in the D.S.Senanayake Memorial School. Their life was peaceful and smooth. They could speak Sinhalese fluently. They were not interested in politics. Most of his friends were Sinhalese.

Jagan did not remember anything being said in his house about Tamil politics. His life revolved around his school, his house, and the temple. Simple and serene.

Suddenly, an earthquake called the '83 riots struck. It was a turning point in the lives of millions of people like him. Everything was changed in a matter of a few moments.

The lives of innocent people became 'unnatural.' For the Tamils, 'unnatural' turned out

I am the Lord

to be 'natural'. One's belongings being stolen right under one's nose; houses being burnt; huddled together in hiding fearing even to breathe, relying on the sympathy of the neighbouring slum rowdies; watching helplessly one's dear ones being disgraced and molested — those atrocities could never be forgotten!

When the riots subsided, they stayed in the camp at the Hindu College, Bambalapitiya; then, as refugees in their own land, they were taken by sea to Jaffna; though even strangers helped them in Jaffna, they could not digest others imposing themselves in their domestic affairs, accustomed as they were to life in Colombo. Such new and bitter experiences continued to plague them.

Later, they went to India and then migrated to Australia; thankfully, once again, his life continued more or less peacefully.

Time is a great mind-healer. As the years passed, his wounds and scars gradually healed. Having been educated in Australia and gallivanted with Australian friends, his thinking too became similar to that of an Australian youth.

Although his father and his friends tried to teach the younger generation the values of Tamil schooling and culture, the latter realized that if they wished to be part of the Australian society and live there, they had to think like the Australians.

His uncle was a doctor in Sydney. He often said, "It is not enough to divide the human brain into left and right. It should also be divided into East and West brain. For instance, let us assume that a doctor is ill with fever. In our country, nurses would immediately prepare coffee or tea for him. Here, they would first ask, 'If the doctor himself has fever, can he meet his patients? Will the patients also be infected with this fever? Will the doctor's skill be affected by his illness?' This illustrates the two different attitudes and approaches."

Accustomed, as he was to such thinking, the hospitality and the loving liberty with which he was treated in India, appeared novel to him.

"Have your bath and come for lunch." Her 'order' cut short his reflections. His family had long ago stopped telling him what he should do. Following the policy of individual freedom, even parents would not advise their children. However, the children invariably expected that they should be taken care of until they were capable of fending for themselves. This was especially so with Asian children who depended on their parents for their university education. Most countries did not offer free education like Sri Lanka. Hence, most students had to work on holidays and do part-time jobs to support themselves and continue studying. However, immigrants from Asian countries were lucky to enjoy the liberty of Western culture and the support of their parents — the best of both worlds.

I am the Lord

He had his bath and was about to sit for lunch, when his father's friend Raghuraman Thanikachalam entered.

Beginning with the question, "How are your parents and sister?" he enquired about their present condition, the children's education, and several other matters.

On being asked, "How long will you be here?" Jagan answered that he would be in Chennai for a few days, and then go on a tour of South India, and that he would stay in Tamil Nadu for six weeks. He said that he would be going first to Mahabalipuram and Kanchipuram near Chennai. Though he grew up in Australia, he had read historical novels written by Kalki, Sandilyan, Akilan, and others. He had long cherished the desire to tread the paths of the Tamil kings of the Pallava, Chola, and Pandiya dynasties. Therefore, he said that he was keen to visit Mahabalipuram the very next day, and Kanchipuram the day after.

Refusing Raghuraman's offer to arrange for a cab, Jagan said he wished to travel as an ordinary passenger by the public transport buses. How could one understand the soil and people of a land, from the luxurious interior of an air-conditioned glass prison called a taxi? His plan was to see and savour the sacred land as one with the crowd.

# 3

Also called Kadalmallai and Mamallapuram, Mahabalipuram is a world wonder. The epics sculpted in stone 1300 years ago by the Pallava kings continue to attract people from all corners of the world, who marvel at their excellence. Having somehow escaped from the ravages of time, not losing the nuances of art, making viewers wonder, these temples and sculptures have withstood the onslaughts of the sea, soil erosions, floods, rms, severe droughts, forest fires, and similar attacks of Mother Nature; even when subjected to alien religions, cultures and fanatics who decried idol worship they are still towering majestic. These epics in stone stand testimony to the Tamils' skills of sculpture, architecture, and knowledge of engineering.

These artistic pieces also testify the truth that men whose lifetime is restricted to just a hundred years, can live for thousands of years through their timeless creations.

The moment he got down from the bus, tourist guides and petty traders surrounded him as birds do fruit-laden trees. Only then did Jagan realize his mistake of having worn jeans and shirt. His facial expression, body language, and dress proclaimed the fact that he was a foreigner. By the time he

I am the Lord

extricated himself from this commercial crowd, and reached the stone statues, he was exasperated.

As he had already read a lot about these statues and sculptures, Jagan was able to appreciate them without anyone's help. Human civilization is inextricably associated with water. History tells us that human settlements flourished wherever rivers flowed. Estuaries where rivers such as the Nile, Euphrates, Tigris, Sind and the Yellow river or the Yangtze flow into the ocean formed the cradles of civilizations. Only after man, who had lived in the forests, as hunter-gatherer, settled in one place and learnt to plough and cultivate crops, did culture, religion, art, literature, philosophy, and science develop.

Thus, because rivers and civilization were closely knit, it is not surprising that descriptions of rivers occupy an important part of the literature created by man.

Our scriptures tell us that the river Cauvery was born when the Tamil Lord Muruga toppled the cruel belonging to the great saint Agastya, who brought Tamil to this world. The Cauvery has sustained the Thanjavur delta as the granary of the south! This very same Cauvery has also been the bone of contention for long between Karnataka and Tamil Nadu. Water is the elixir of life. In the hands of unscrupulous politicians, water is also a weapon!

There is a Hindu myth about the origin of the river Ganges. The epics say that it was as the result of the arduous penance of Bhageerathan that the Ganges was brought to the earth from heaven. As it could cause an immense flood if it flowed on to the earth in its entirety, it fell on the head of Lord Siva, seated on Mount Kailas, and then flowing through His tresses, divided into several branches and reached the earth.

This 'herculean' effort made by Bhageerathan, to immerse his forefathers' ashes in water, continues to be referred to as Bhageerathan's effort in current parlance.

Some argue that the yogi standing on one leg doing penance is not Bhageerathan, and it is Arjuna, who engaged in such an action during the war mentioned in the Mahabharatha, to request Lord Siva for the deadly weapon, Pasupathaastram. The sculpture depicting this is still referred to as Arjuna's penance.

What did the sculptor have in mind, when he used his chisel as a writer does his pen? Whatever it may be, he would never even have dreamt that scholars of a later generation would offer their own interpretations of his creation, and obtain their M.Litt or Ph.D degrees!

Lost in reflections such as these, and in the gravitational laws of physics, which prevented the huge globular stone called Krishna's Butter Ball from rolling down, he reached the Trimurthi temple.

I am the Lord

Built to house the Trinity of Birth, Sustenance and Death, Lord Brahma, Vishnu and Siva, the Trimurthi temple stood as a testimony to the great truth, that life was a circle and that death was as important as birth. Jagan realized that birth and death were cyclical. Only when the old order changes, it yields place to the new. Otherwise, the universe will become static, changeless. This is what the Tamils meant when they said, 'ring out the old, and ring in the new'. Bhogi, celebrated the day before Pongal, also indicates this. Temples for Brahma are rare. However, the Pallava king who built this temple seems to have been aware of this great philosophy.

Fascinated by the sculptures of elephants, lions, oxen and several other animals scattered around majestically, he climbed the lighthouse, and turning 360° like a bird, took in the unsurpassed beauties of the Pallavas. Among the gigantic sculptures of animals created by the great kings, is the awesome temple of Mahishamardhini, that resembles a huge beast sleeping. When viewed from the lighthouse, the huge rock appeared like the body of the sleeping beast, and the pillared hall of the cave and the temple thereon, appeared like its head. Admiring the incomparable creations of the Pallava kings, he reached the chariots of the Panchapandavas. Said to be equal to the cave temples of Ajanta and Ellora, and built in the architectural style of the Buddhists, these temples too were carved out of individual rocks. As the sanctums of these temples were empty, they gave rise to several assumptions.

Ezhuth Aani

Most of the temples in the complex were carved out of individual rocks and are referred to as cave temples. However, the Shore temple goes onestep further, and stands testimony to the architectural excellence of the Pallavas. It stands as an unexcelled example of the Dravidian temple structure, supposed to be the forerunner of the magnificent Cholas' Big temple of Thanjavur, and the similar one at Gangaikonda Cholapuram, that consist of the sanctum sanctorum, corridors, tower, and outer walls. It is assumed to be one of the seven shore temples of Mamallapuram. It was also a place sanctified by a verse sung by Thirumangai Azhwar in his Peria Thirumozhi. He describes Mamallapuram as Kadalmallai harbour, in which rows of ships laden with wealth and elephants, are struggling to free themselves from their anchors in the midst of the waves. The Italian travel writer, Marco Polo, has described it as the shore of the seven pagodas. Of these seven, only one has survived. The rest are believed to have been swallowed by the sea, and to be lying under the sea even today.

It was 11 p.m. by the time Jagan had dinner and went to bed, on his return to Chennai. The various sights of Mamallapuram reminded him of the ancient greatness of the Tamils.

# 4

"Where is Jagan? He left in the morning. He has not returned yet. They say there has been an explosion. Can't understand what is going on," said Seethalamma, worried. It was over the phone that Thanikachalam, who was still in his shop in Pondy Bazaar doing business, heard his wife's lament.

"Yes. Some bomb blast at an election meeting, it seems. They say Rajiv Gandhi has been hurt. Where has Jagan gone? He returned very late even last night, didn't he? An educated youth, he'll return somehow".

Though he reassured his wife, Thanikachalam was inwardly very anxious. He knew quite well that if something were to happen to his friend's son, he would have to shoulder the responsibility. As time passed, news of Rajiv Gandhi's assassination began to spread like wild fire.

Thanikachalam's family was one of the thousands of families of Indian origin, which had been taken by the British colonialists to Ceylon. They had sacrificed their blood and sweat, and contributed to the fertility of the tea and rubber plantations in the hills established by the British on Sri Lankan soil. It was due to their labour that Sri Lanka flourished in the tea and rubber industries, and progressed economically to the envy of the other Asian countries. However, just before independence, in the first parliamentary elections, they used their voting rights to strengthen the Leftist parties, and emerged as a counter force to the capitalists. Hence, after independence, these Tamil hill country people became the first victims of the ethnic hatred of the Sinhalese. They were stripped of their citizenship and voting rights overnight, and they became stateless. Many of them who had become victims of those in power, lost their statehood and facing an uncertain future, returned to their homeland. One of those was Thanikachalam's father.

Though he had come back to his homeland and begun life anew, he maintained contact with Sri Lanka. This had continued until Jagan's generation.

Later, during the '83 riots, when Jagan's family was driven into exile as the sacrificial lambs of the next stage of ethnic exclusivity, it was Thanikachalam's father who offered them shelter; this helped to continue the bond between the two families to the next generation.

First, the Tamils of Indian origin, then the European mixed race called Burgers, and finally, the Sri Lankan Tamils; thus, having driven away everyone, what was called the Pearl of the Indian Ocean was turned into the 'tear drop' of the Indian Ocean by the Sinhalese Buddhist dominant fanaticism! Many wondered when it would turn its wrath on the Muslims!

I am the Lord

When Indira Gandhi was the Prime Minister, the Tamils had hopes that somehow she would solve this problem. Exerting military pressure on the one hand, by providing the Tamil youth weapons and military training, she also engaged in a dialogue (with Sri Lanka) through experienced statesmen like Parthasarathi.

Unfortunately, however, before she could achieve her goal with respect to the Tamils, Indira was shot dead by Sikh militants.

For the sole reason that he was the son of Indira Gandhi, Rajiv became the Prime Minister, though he had neither an understanding of the current political scenario, nor any experience in politics. Soon, he removed his mother's loyalist statesmen and selected as his advisors less experienced 'officials' like Romesh Bhandari, who had absolutely no knowledge of the Tamils' problem. He then hurriedly signed the Indolanka pact, only to find that he was no match for the wily old fox, J. R. Jeyawardane. Finally, he suffered an ignominious insult, like the ape that pulled the wedge with the Tamils ending up fighting against the army of the very India, which they worshipped as their motherland.

Embroiled in the Bofors scandal and facing other corruption charges, he lost the elections, and very soon became the ex-PM.

As a reincarnation, he had once again entered the election fray, portraying himself as a prodigal son.

Who would have killed Rajiv Gandhi? Would there be any connection between this and Jagan's disappearance? In the midst of several questions such as these, Thanikachalam got in touch with his police friends over the phone.

Jagan's travel to Kanchipuram by an ordinary bus, his not returning home, the bomb blast that same night at Sriperambudur on the way - the very thought of all these, churned Thanikachalam's stomach.

Was there any connection between Jagan and this bomb blast, by any chance? Thanikachalam felt as if his head would burst. As far as he knew, there was no link between Jagan and the Sri Lankan Tamil revolution; there was no possibility either. He had left Sri Lanka after the '83 riots; he had come to India with his family; and from here, he had gone to Australia. Reports coming from there suggested that he was focused on his progress through education. There was no chance, under the circumstances, for him to be involved in the insurgency. Though his rational mind said this, he could not reject the possibility that Jagan may have links with militancy despite his alienation from his motherland, just as the Sikhs living in Canada carried out the Air India bomb blast. Thanikachalam was utterly confused. As for

Seethalammal, she was worried as to what she would say to Jagan's parents.

That night, none in that house slept. Unable to decide whether to inform Jagan's parents over the phone, Thanikachalam was under terrible stress. Life throws up several such situations. Should one raise the alarm now or not? Many have faced the dilemma of whether to alert everyone and then feel sheepish (for having made a mountain out of a molehill), or procrastinate and pave the way to a great disaster.

When Jagan did not appear until the next night too, Thanikachalam realized the imperative need to somehow inform his parents.

# 5

"**D**id he tell you the places he intended to visit?" was the first question that Jagan's father asked Thanikachalam, the moment he landed at the Chennai airport. Boarding a taxi, they first went to the T'Nagar police station.

"I'm sorry, my friend. We never expected such a thing to happen," said Thanikachalam, looking at the ground, guiltily. It was three days since Jagan's disappearance.

During the '83 riots, innumerable mothers, and fathers lost their children. In the war that followed too, thousands of young lives were lost. Having escaped from all this, and gone to a different country, should one lose one's son like this? What a tragedy is this?

"We've informed all the police stations. We'll find him somehow," assured the inspector.

"Don't go there alone searching for him. Preliminary investigations have led our officers to suspect that this might be the work of the Sri Lankan Tamils. We believe that this bomb blast has been executed in the same manner as the one by which Padmanabha was murdered on Tamil Nadu's soil. Hence, we are forced to see all Sri Lankan Tamils as suspects, for the time being. Jagan is not an exception to this. If you go there without police permission, we may have to arrest you too."

These words of the inspector were like a bull stamping a man who had already fallen on the ground.

"We are also Tamils; don't let us down like this," said Jagan's father, in an imploring tone.

"I'm an Indian first, only then a Tamilian. That too, a police officer," said the inspector, keenly watching those sitting in front of him.

"Our former Prime Minister and the last scion of the Nehru family has been assassinated. We believe that the Sri Lankan Tamils are involved in this. Coincidentally, your son has been missing since that day. Our first task will be to find out if there is any connection between this murder and your son. Even if we do find him, we'll have to interrogate him."

The officer who said this with a blank face, continued, "You go home. If we have any information, we'll certainly contact Mr Thanikachalam." He then sent them off.

The next few days passed in telephone conversations, and in watching TV news bulletins, which consisted of exciting police enquiries and chasing of criminals. In the meanwhile, though they met both the DMK and ADMK politicians, it was clear to them, that these regional politicians were merely 'mike' wielding 'speech' heroes, not action heroes.

Days passed. It was time to report for work again. As all the newspapers printed Sivarasan's photograph, the people of Tamil Nadu realized that this was the work of a Sri Lankan Tamils' group.

Subsequently, when all sympathy for the Sri Lankan Tamils had dried up, the investigations proceeded only from the perspective that Jagan was a militant. The police were fully engrossed in finding the murderers, and refused to even consider the possibility that an innocent man could have disappeared. The investigating officers carried out their duties like sniffer dogs.

As the days passed, only stories about the search for Sivarasan continued to be circulated. In course of time, Thanikachalam himself began to doubt whether Jagan could be a militant. In case he was involved in Rajiv's murder, Thanikachalam feared that his own business might be sealed, for having given asylum to Jagan. He conveyed his fear discreetly to his friend.

With the passage of several weeks, and his efforts at finding Jagan proving to be as futile as banging one's head against a wall, it was imperative for Jagan's father to return to Australia.

I am the Lord

# 6

Faith is the foundation of life. Ups and downs alternate in every man's life. The same may be said of trials and tribulations.

There are many who are engaged in what are called Mcjobs, that is, jobs in which there is no scope for any progress. For some, earning their daily bread itself is a challenge. If one were to get all his needs fulfilled at will, he will begin to covet others' wealth.

In some countries, the very survival of oneself and one's relatives becomes a problem.

But, whatever the difficulty, if one has the conviction that tomorrow will bring a new dawn, it will be easy to bear today's burden. Thus, even those who have no food to eat, spend their money visiting temples and other religious shrines. The belief or illusion that those who suffer in this life will be rewarded in the next is what has preserved the fabric of society. Otherwise, one revolution or the other would have eliminated the rich long ago.

It is clear from the number of lottery tickets sold every day in India, how people are being deceived by the commercialization of hope. Even in the greatest capitalist country of America, there are numerous rags-to-riches stories. When the time is favourable, opportunities come knocking at one's door. But the majority of men do not realize the truth that only those who seize hold of the opportunities offered to them and work hard, will prosper; they waste their time day-dreaming that they too will hit the jackpot one day. Howsoever, members of Jagan's family continued their life in Australia in the hope that he would return home one day.

A telephonic message that arrived one day sounded the death-knell of all their hopes.

It was Thanikachalam who spoke. The news, "The police have found Jagan's torn passport," struck them like a thunderbolt.

This passport had been found only after the authorities had combed the Sriperambudur area repeatedly. Nearly everyone connected with the murder had been either arrested or killed, or committed suicide. In these circumstances, it was not known whether Jagan was in any way involved in the murder, or he was killed in the explosion as an innocent spectator. However, the police inspector had said that for a small consideration, the investigation regarding Jagan's implication in the terrorist attack could be expedited, and for a bigger amount, his death certificate could be provided. Left with no other option, Jagan's family shelled out money to speed up the investigation, as to whether Jagan was a militant, but categorically refused to accept his death certificate.

With the certificate, they would get the insurance pay out. "Was it for currency notes that we begot and brought up our son?" they asked, adamantly.

Jagan's mother visited the Murugan temple at Sydney every Friday and performed poojas. When the pooja was being performed in his name, and the priest asked, "Where is your son, madam?" she would say that he was studying in India. She said the same thing to the neighbours and relatives. Though they sensed something tragic, they accepted her word, not having the courage to enquire about it directly.

# 7

A series of shells battered Kabul city. Jagan's camp was fifty kilometres away from the city. As the summer heat increased gradually, the climate was pleasant. Having completed his sentry duty and his night prayers, he lay in his allotted bed, and recollected the events of the past eleven months.

Spending the whole day sightseeing in Kanchipuram, he was on his way back to Chennai, when a group of Congress workers (hooligans) stopped the bus and took them all to attend the meeting to be addressed by Rajiv Gandhi. He too, was eager to see Rajiv, and hence, went willingly. They were all given food packets. That is the Indian political culture.

Though several leaders spoke eloquently, there was no sign of Rajiv. It was novel and amusing for him, to see the people waiting patiently, without worrying about the passage of time. The compulsion of having to move away from a hectic world and put up with a leisurely life began that day itself for Jagan. Subsequent events appeared like a movie to him even now. As he stood, one with the crowd, the earth shook with a big bang. It was as if a thousand lightning struck simultaneously. Such 'mega' brightness! Unaware of what had happened, people ran helterskelter; he too followed them. In the mad rush that ensued, he lost his wallet and passport. With the few Indian currency notes he had in his hand, he boarded a bus not knowing where it was bound, and somehow left the place called Sriperambudur.

Merely because they wanted to leave that place, many had got into the bus, without knowing where it was bound. After about an hour's journey, it was stopped in front of a police checkpoint in Andhra Pradesh.

Amidst the bus passengers who, until then, had had no idea of what had happened, a rumour began to spread that Rajiv had been injured. Some said it was the work of Islamic militants, while the others claimed that it might have been the work of the Naxalites. As they spoke in a different dialect of Tamil and Telugu, he could not fully understand what they said.

At this juncture, the police entered the bus, asked all of them to get down, and began to scour the bus. They detained three passengers who could not prove their identity, and made them sit on the floor in the checkpoint.

Jagan was one of the three. The man who translated the policeman's questions from Telugu to Tamil, made it clear to the policeman that Jagan was a foreigner, as soon as he opened his mouth to reply. As he had neither his passport nor any other document to prove his identity, the police eyed him with suspicion.

Ezhuth Aani

The bus dropped the three of them at the checkpoint on the wayside, and went on its way. Distressed at not knowing why he was detained, and not having any proof of his foreign status, Jagan felt even more helpless at his inability to explain his condition to the policemen, who did not know Tamil. To make matters worse, the policemen's knowledge of English was poor, while Jagan's English accent was beyond their understanding. Thus, he was unable to explain his predicament to them.

As soon as it dawned, and the sun peeped through the clouds, they put him in a vehicle.

All the suspects were put in a large 'lock-up' camp. Ordinary criminals as well as those who had no proof of their identity, like Jagan, were confined together.

For Jagan, who had had no food or water until that afternoon, the bread and gravy given to him later were like nectar. Accustomed to eating bread with vegemite, margarine and jam, the credit for making Jagan crave for plain bread and more of that bland gravy, should be given to his hunger.

After that, he was given a mat. Used to a hectic Western lifestyle, here he was, lying on a mat spread on the ground, and forced to count the tiles on the roof. What cruelty! How many times could he count the tiles?

I am the Lord

When man cannot change his fate, he must learn to console himself and survive as best as he can. Were he to count the tiles faster, would the clock too run faster?

Ezhuth Aani

# 8

For the next four days, he was given a quarter pound of bread and gravy or dhal at regular times. There were four others confined along with him in the same room. They appeared to be elderly villagers. They spoke in Telugu among themselves. Even those who knew a few Tamil words struggled to understand his Jaffna Tamil, which had 'worn out' in the course of his life in Australia.

Nevertheless, he managed to comprehend the situation. He was in a small prison in Tirupathi. He also came to know that Rajiv had been murdered, and that a wide net had been cast to apprehend the murderers. He was in a dilemma. That is, if he were to reveal his identity, he might be imprisoned indefinitely, on the assumption that all Sri Lankan Tamils were Liberation Tigers. At the same time, if the authorities did not know who he was, there was a possibility that, accepting a bribe, he may be released in a few months' time, or that his parents would somehow find him.

One by one, those confined along with him, managed to get them released by offering bribes. On the fourth day, he was transferred to another prison. When Jagan attempted to argue in English against the change, all that he got was a series of blows and kicks. Perhaps the officer, who did not

I am the Lord

know English, mistook Jagan's language to be a form of ridicule.

With his hands tied, he was taken along with some others similarly bound, to an unknown destination. About twenty to thirty of them travelled several hours in a bus that did not have any window.

Finally, they were confined in another prison. All of them (except for Jagan) appeared menacing. It was common for these prisoners to grow large beards and moustaches. There were many reasons for this. First, they were given the facility to shave only once a week. Moreover, in a place where everyone sported a moustache, being clean-shaven would be considered feminine, and there was a fear that such men would be subjected to sexual abuse.

One could not go out of the prison. Nevertheless, inside, the prisoners had their say. Soon Jagan realized that there was a sort of order in the atrocities that took place in the prison. The prisoners had formed themselves into groups. Among these groups, there was hierarchy of authority. Though they were mostly respectful towards the prison warden, Mr Gupta, there were a few thugs who behaved disrespectfully even towards him. First, Jagan was taken to the prison warden. Gupta knew a little English. He asked the former what his name was. When he said, 'Jagan', he asked, "Where are you from?" When he said, "Australia," he laughed so heartily that his moustache moved up and down, as did his paunch.

Ezhuth Aani

In response to his question, "Why do you laugh?" he was slapped forcefully. "Don't ask me questions," said Gupta, as he pressed his booted leg on Jagan, who had fallen down. After allowing him to be suffocated for some time, he removed his foot.

Then, as though he had transgressed a tradition, he hurriedly lifted Jagan by his collar, and slapped him repeatedly.

"You do not have a passport. There is none to question me, if I were to kill you. I can imprison you indefinitely on charges of complicity with the assassins of our former prime minister, Rajiv Gandhi. I can also let the other prisoners feed on you like dogs on their prey. There are AIDS patients too in this prison. They will tear you to pieces. After that, you will also contract HIV."

For the next two days, Jagan was subjected to different kinds of torture. He had no other alternative but to submit himself to the sexual abuse inflicted on him by the officer, Gupta. Ignominies, which he had not even dreamt of in his life, were imposed on him. Whenever Gupta abused him sexually, he suffered unbearable pain. But with the fear that he might be handed over to the other rascally prisoners, and his helplessness at the realization that he had no other alternative, his resentment gradually decreased. The decrease was only physical. Mentally, he continued to feel dirty. A prison should be like a school, refining a man so that he can integrate himself usefully in society, and be a deterrent to others not to commit crimes that are punishable by law. On the contrary, the prison here was a jungle, where men indulged their animal instincts freely, stripped of the garb of civilization. For Jagan who was brought up in a very protective disciplined societal set up, these circumstances induced suicidal ideation. He managed to remain patient, suppressing thoughts of self-harm. Relegating the ideas of self-respect and prestige to the background, his main daily concern was how to escape from the torture and survive. Life is a school, they say; every day we learn our lessons, it is said. What Jagan learnt in his prison days was, how humanitarianism could be degenerated, and to what level! The little belief that he had in God, deserted him. Had a God really existed, He would have terminated the injustice that was perpetrated unbridled, long ago!

After some time, Jagan who had been in solitary confinement was allowed to interact with the other prisoners during mealtimes. As he was considered Gupta's property, nobody else took liberties with him.

In course of time, he gained 'his' acquaintance. His white dress, fez cap and beard, identified him as a Muslim. A group always surrounded him. His face was pacific; at the same time, his unshakable self-confidence and determination were obvious.

With a heavy heart and without talking to anyone, Jagan was having his meal alone. Since his imprisonment, he had been avoiding non-vegetarian food. This was because he was not used to eating meat right from childhood. Hence, he avoided non-vegetarian dishes. Seeing this, the Elder came close to him and said, "Friend, God has created these animals for man to eat. Why don't you eat them?" Their conversation, which started thus, lasted some time. He spoke English fluently. Hence, Jagan poured out his whole history to him.

Hesitantly, he narrated how the prison warden Gupta abused him sexually. Jagan had developed an inexplicable trust and respect for the Muslim Elder.

# 9

Within the next few days, Jagan was accepted as a member of the Elder's group. The Muslim youth who were with him, were fearless. The other prisoners had a kind of respect mixed with fear, for them.

Once when Gupta tried to misbehave again with Jagan, he was beaten black and blue. After that, nobody disturbed Jagan. He spoke to the Elder several times on several topics.

Initially, the Elder who was eager to know about Jagan, gradually began to open up and disclose details about himself.

Jagan had told him his entire story. How his peaceful childhood had been turned topsy-turvy by the 1983 riots, as if by a cyclone; how, like birds scattering in different directions when a woodcutter cuts the tree which holds them, the Tamils had run for their lives; how, recently his Indian journey had been cut short by a bomb blast, and how he had suffered imprisonment - all this Jagan narrated in full detail to the Elder. Having listened patiently, he introduced himself as Maulana Taariq.

"Brother, you have suffered so much. Do you know why?" he asked.

Jagan replied, "I don't understand anything."

"It was Buddhism that destroyed your race in '83. What is ironical about this is the fact that Buddhism advocates peace. However today, in many countries where the majority of people follow Buddhism, it is violence that is dominant. Most importantly, in countries like Sri Lanka, Cambodia, Vietnam, and Myanmar, where the Theravada Buddhists live, human life has no value. Similarly, people do not have freedom of speech. What you see today is the ugly face of politics-oriented Buddhism.

"When King Ashoka won the battle at Kalinga, a Buddhist monk boldly reviewed the king's victory, and pointing out the destruction caused by the war, changed his mind so that he became a peace-lover. Is there such a monk today? Buddhist monks have lost the Buddha and the peace-loving ways that he preached, for the sake of political power and authority. This is the state of affairs now.

"Don't think therefore, that your Hinduism is an unblemished superior religion. Caught in the vicious grip of Brahminism, Hinduism established the dominance of the Brahmins, by imposing upon people the cruel caste distinctions of the so-called Varnashrama Dharma. In both Hinduism and Judaism, one's status in society is determined unjustly by one's birth. Just as Christianity as a religion was born 'in revolt' against the dominance

I am the Lord

of the Pharisees of Judaism, Buddhism arose out of the rebellion against the dominance of the Brahmins in Hinduism. Buddhism advocates equality and justice. It is not one's birth that determines one's status in life. Buddhism reiterates that one's status is decided by one's deeds, education and so on. Buddhism permits anyone to become a religious head.

"Buddhism was established only for the sake of those who wished to follow its principles fully as a way of life, and as an instrument of motivation and guidance. In course of time, in their desire to share power and authority, the monks have joined hands with the political bosses and are holding sway.

"In 1837, an Englishman named George Turnour, translated, and published the epic *Mahavamsa*, supposed to have been written by the Sri Lankan, Mahanama Thero. This was very helpful later, to support the argument that Sri Lanka belonged only to the Sinhalese. The Buddhist monks, who wrote this *Mahavamsa*, lived in the biggest and oldest vihara called the Mahavihara. Under the patronage of the kings, these monks began to live in luxury, wielding great influence. Using their political clout, they succeeded in re-establishing a kind of Brahminism, very similar to the one, which Buddha had broken free from. You and your family were scorched by the huge fire lit by these Buddhist monks in Sri Lanka."

So saying, Maulana asked, "Do you know that at one time Buddhism had flourished in the whole of India?"

"No; please tell me," said Jagan.

"For several centuries, Buddhism held sway over the whole of India. Not only India, but also the whole of Asia accepted Buddhism. People welcomed the fresh air of equality and brotherhood, which was the Buddhist code, as against the stifling dominance of the Brahmins. But today, Buddhism has almost disappeared from India, where it was born. Do you know why?

"The Hindus tried various tricks to bring back the Brahmins' dominance. They accepted Lord Buddha as a Hindu God, the reincarnation of Lord Vishnu. They integrated many of the tenets of Buddhism into Hinduism. Adi Sankara preached the philosophy of Advaitha, which was almost another version of Mahayana Buddhism. Apart from this, in your Tamil Nadu itself, the Bhakti movement became popular in the 6th and 7th centuries. The songs that were sung by the four Hindu saints Sambandar, Appar,, Sundarar and Manickavasagar and the Vaishnavaite Azhwars inspired the people to worship God with renewed fervour. Moreover, violence erupted against the Buddhists. The Buddha viharas were either demolished or converted into Hindu temples. Buddhism was totally eradicated from India. People who had embraced Buddhism were re-integrated into Hinduism. However, the Brahmins

I am the Lord

continued to maintain caste distinctions, using new connotations.

"Though the religious epics and Thevarams (devotional songs) were in circulation among people, the Vedas and mantras were handed down by oral tradition from one generation to another only among the Brahmins; other castes were not given the opportunity to learn or chant them.

"Knowledge is Power, was the motto strongly followed by the Brahmin fundamentalists. They made knowledge solely theirs. Hence, they claimed that only THEY were qualified to perform religious rites and rituals, and chant the mantras. They proclaimed that receiving charity was their birth right, and thus they enhanced their economic status.

"Even the Thevarams were inscribed on palm-leaves, and preserved for many centuries secretly by the Brahmins. Much later, it was only during the reign of Raja Raja Chola, through the efforts of Nambiandar Nambi, that the possibility arose for others to access them.

"Do you know that the Bhagavad Gita itself advocates the observance of caste distinctions? Caste violence has been practiced in the name of God Himself, in many places. Take, for example, the story of Ekalaiva, one of the best characters in the Mahabharatha. It narrates how meanly Ekalaiva's thumb was cut off, merely to prevent a low caste man from equalling the high caste Arjuna in archery. Thus, the people were deluded into believing in the superiority of the Brahmins. Later, Europeans like Max Muller gathered various details about the Hindu religion, gave it due recognition in the Western world, and propagated the intellectual fraud.

"You have been affected by that Hindutva. Buddhist fundamentalism on one-hand and Hindu atrocities on the other, have ruined you.

"Hindu fanaticism has impacted the whole of India today. Its ugly face has been exposed clearly to the world, through the incidents that took place in Ayodhya and Mathura. The atrocities committed to suppress the people in Kashmir, and the government- sponsored terrorism unleashed in the Punjab, are also dark pages in the history of Hinduism."

Pausing suddenly in his discourse, he asked, "Do you know why several Hindus embraced Islam and continue to do so?"

Jagan replied, "Historians say that during their successive invasions, the Muslims converted many Hindus at knife-point."

"What you know is only half the truth. Muslims took up arms only to protect themselves during the wars of the Crusade, and to prevent Christian attacks. It is true that Islam spread in India at knifepoint. That is not the only reason for the spread of Islam in India. Buddhism was driven

I am the Lord

out of India by the cunning ways practiced by the intelligent Brahmins.

"Later, when Islam came to India, with its doctrine of equality and brotherhood, many Hindus enthusiastically embraced the new religion.

"The largest Muslim country in the world is Indonesia. Islam spread there without any war or violence. From this, the fact can be understood, that Islam did not spread only by wielding weapons.

"Today, many Christians in the West are embracing the religion of the Muslims. Islam is spreading fast. No power can prevent this."

Maulana then began to talk about various details pertaining to Jagan with interest. Their friendship grew. There was a kind of mutual understanding between them. The Elder did not compel him to convert to Islam. However, gradually Maulana's and his friends' customs infected Jagan also. He joined their group as a member. When they prayed, they did not compel him also to pray. Through their support, he was rid of the harassment of Gupta and the other thugs. Days passed thus in prison. Uncertain of what would happen tomorrow, today was lived for its own sake. When the end is unknown, the present becomes the future. Do caged birds, deprived of their freedom, spend their lives like this? Only now, Jagan realized how fortunate he had been in Australia, roaming about freely as he liked! As the days passed, his longing to breathe the air of freedom acquired gigantic proportions.

I am the Lord

# 10

"**M**y friend, I must tell you something. It is a great secret. You must keep it to yourself. If anyone else comes to know about it, your life will be in danger."

He spoke softly. However, the tone of his words inspired fear.

"We have planned to escape from here. You can come with us. If you don't want to, you can stay in this prison itself. Nobody knows how long this imprisonment will last. You must tell me your decision within a few hours." Maulana Taariq will speak only after deliberation; he will act only after planning.

Jagan reflected deeply. Without the support of Maulana and his friends, his life would undoubtedly be deplorable. If he were to be caught once again in the clutches of Gupta and the other thugs, he may have to suffer worse torture. He knew only too well that he would never get justice or clemency. He may have to live a slave all his life. There was every chance of his being afflicted with AIDS. When he thought of the torture that he suffered at the hands of Gupta, his heartbeat rose and beads of perspiration appeared on his forehead. The thought of being caught in this endless hell, produced in him a sort of unimaginable dark despair. He felt as if he were in the grip of an illusion, that the outside world had forgotten him, and he had no other alternative but to languish in that prison all his life. The thought that even if he were to die nobody would know or worry about it, horrified him.

He analysed his condition. It was not possible to remain here. The other option was to betray Maulana and his group, by exposing them. The very thought of betrayal made him feel ashamed and disgusted with himself. He rejected forthwith the idea of exposing Maulana, who had saved and protected him. Moreover, after betraying the Elder, there was no guarantee that he would be granted freedom or shown any mercy. On the contrary, Maulana and his group would take revenge on him from within the prison itself. It was quite evident that after such an act, his condition would be like that of a betel nut caught in the middle of a nutcracker.

As time passed, it became clear to him that the only option open to him was to escape. If he escaped with Maulana, he could reach the outside world. He could also become 'the most wanted' by the Indian government. He concluded that come what may, he must somehow escape from this place of torture. He felt like laughing at his own plight. It was like that of a piece of fish caught between the burning fire and the boiling oil. He consoled himself with the thought, that his plight was much better than that of those who, at a much younger age, suffered difficulties and losses much greater than his.

I am the Lord

On approaching Maulana with this mind-set, the Elder observed him keenly.

"Can I trust you?"

"Absolutely.

"Right. Do as I say. There is nothing more to tell you now. When our friends from outside give the signal, we shall start our operation. You don't have to do anything. Be ready to come with us when I tell you."

After looking at him sharply for some time, he asked, "Do you remember what I told you then? If this plan leaks out, I cannot give you any assurance for your life." He said this in a calm but firm voice.

The days that followed, instilled in him great confidence and raised his expectations. Maulana spoke to him as usual about various things and not about the jailbreak attempt.

Almost a week passed. Suddenly one day, an explosive sound shattered the stillness of the night. Gupta's screams were heard; but soon there was silence. The characteristic sounds of doors being banged and locks being broken open appeared like a musical night orchestra.

Realizing that his time had arrived, Jagan changed into his only pants and was ready. As the power supply to the prison had been cut, he could not see anything. Suddenly, he heard his door being opened and some men with torchlights beckoning him. Knowing that it was Maulana calling him, he followed.

Silently, they proceeded, walking and running. The compound wall of the prison had been broken by the collision of some vehicle. In that place, its height was low enough for them to jump over. Once again their journey continued, running and walking, amidst bushes and shrubs, for several miles. That night was, indeed, a long one for Jagan.

After they had covered many miles on foot, they got into a waiting jeep. There were eight of them in that group, including Maulana. That jeep bore the identification marks of a government department. Crossing dense forests and rocky terrains, they finally managed to reach a house. Men in army uniforms guarded it.

The blackness of the night was replaced by the light red of the early dawn. The youth there spoke to Maulana in a language unknown to Jagan. As they used only the English word 'comrade' often, he guessed rightly that they were probably Marxists who had come together with Maulana's group as companions, in their effort to achieve a common goal.

# 11

They were forced to be in hiding in that house for several days. For communication purposes, they taught him a few Telugu and Hindi words. All of them engaged themselves in physical exercise every day. Maulana's men offered prayers five times a day. The others appeared to be disinterested in any religion whatsoever. For the sake of mutual interests, two groups professing two entirely different political ideologies helped each other.

The house nestled and hidden in the dense forest had only the basic amenities. All of them shared the essential duties such as cleaning the house, hunting, and procuring food items from the villagers. The rest of the group viewed Jagan only with suspicion. He realized that but for Maulana's support and patronage, they would have considered him a burden and eliminated him long ago.

That house did not have power supply and drinking water. Water had to be fetched from a small spring some distance away.

After many days, Jagan was allowed to carry water, cook, and do sundry jobs. It was a relief for him also, to engage himself in useful work, rather than be a non-productive 'time eater'.

Cut off from the outside world, their daily chores became significant events in their everyday life. Nevertheless, compared to the days spent in the Indian prison, this was like heaven for Jagan.

Maulana had returned after his trip to some place. Jagan met him and asked, "How long are you going to be inactive like this?"

"Inactive like this?" asked Maulana in surprise, looking at him. He then threw an English daily newspaper in front of him. The headline 'The Sri Lankan terrorists responsible for Rajiv Gandhi's murder will soon be caught' stared him in the face. The jailbreak at Anantpur had also been described in detail on the first page. It was reported that twelve Islamic terrorists, three Naxalites, and one Sri Lankan Tamil had escaped.

Moreover, at a time when it was believed that there was a connection between the Lashkar terrorists in Kashmir, the LTTE alias Liberation Tigers, and the Naxalites, this incident seemed to confirm that belief, said the paper. The report also detailed the news that the warden Gupta along with three others, had been killed in the jailbreak, and another terrorist had been shot dead later.

"Look here, Jagan. Things are not well in the country. Until Rajiv's killers are nabbed, police vigilance will be severe. In such circumstances, we cannot travel openly. Remaining quiet in this place, is best for us. When the situation improves, we can go where we want to," said Maulana.

I am the Lord

He continued. "You have been our partner in the jailbreak, knowingly or otherwise. Three security guards have been killed in that incident. Under the circumstances, if the Indian police catch you, their treatment will be more torturous than before. In addition, you will be accused of murder, terrorism and so on, and sentenced to life imprisonment. Just think. Would you like to spend the rest of your life suffering at the hands of cruel sadists like Gupta?"

Jagan remained silent. Maulana said, "I shall help you to leave India. But you should listen to what I say and act accordingly." It was clear that he was interested in Jagan's welfare.

Jagan understood the state of affairs only too well. He had no other alternative. He realized that his condition was similar to that of the Nair who had caught the tiger's tail, in the famous story.

Every day dawned anew; and it brought new challenges. He began to cooperate with the rest of the group whole-heartedly, with the confidence that somehow he could face and overcome those challenges.

Although Jagan had taken refuge under Maulana out of sheer necessity, that is, consequent to his realization of the reality that his safety depended totally on him, and hence, his helplessness, he also recognized the fact that he had great respect and regard for the Elder. On their side, the rebels too realized the truth that if Jagan were to leave them, he would be a potential threat to their safety. Above all, was the feeling that they wanted to be friendly with him, and it was this that prompted them to retain him in their company. Gradually, the others in the group acknowledged Jagan as their friend.

I am the Lord

## 12

**J**agan taught them English. At the same time, he too learnt their philosophy. Maulana warned him not to get too friendly with the Naxalites. "They are atheists. The relationship between them and us, is like train friendship. We have certain common needs. We need a hideout, food, and transport. They need money, arms and so on. We help each other. But we never trust each other beyond a certain limit," he said.

Due to these warnings, Jagan sought the company of the Muslim youth more. They taught him the doctrine of Islam, quite casually.

Allah alone is God. The most important basis of Islam is that there is no other God but Allah. Maulana said, "The moment a person accepts this truth wholeheartedly, he becomes a Muslim. It was on this basis, that the Muslims destroyed the Hindu temples and sculptures, when they invaded India.

"The second basic tenet is that Mohammed (sal) is God's last messenger. Messengers of God are not God. Christians worship the Lord's messenger, Jesus, as the Lord Himself. This is not only wrong, but also against the Lord. Moreover, God sent Mohammed (sal) after Jesus, as the last messenger. God has offered man several truths through His messengers, like Adam, Ibrahim

(Abraham), Moosa (Moses), Dawood (David), and (Isa) Jesus. These teachings can be found in the Bible, scattered and misinterpreted. That is why God sent Mohammed Nabi (sal) as His last messenger. God has blessed him by preaching the Quran to him. The Quran is God's last and only book that has no mistakes. Man has modified the others.

"The third belief is that the Quran is the final and flawless book blessed by God. The fourth is that Muslims believe firmly that there is a Day of Judgment."

As Jagan comprehended all this, Maulana asked him, "Do you think that Mohammed (sal) who never had any schooling could have written the Quran all by himself?

"No, no! This is God's grace! The Quran was written, verse by verse, for twenty-three years, as preached by God to His servant, Jibreel.

"Islam is the only religion that recognizes all the messengers of God. The Jews believe in Moses, but not in Jesus. Christians believe in Jesus, but not in Mohammed Nabi (sal). Islam alone believes in all the messengers of God' said Maulana, and remained silent for some time.

"Remember one thing. The Day of Judgment will soon come. On that Day, the dead will be resurrected. After the Judgment is given, the Good will enter Heavenly bliss. The rest will go to Hell. All those who do not follow Allah will go to Hell.

"Everything is ordained by God. Long ago, it was decided by God that you should join me. We believe that man acts according to God's will. However, man has been given limited freedom. If he chooses the ways of sin, he will be ruined. For example, God's will brings you to me. Even now, you may choose to leave if you wish. If you do so, however, nobody can save you from disaster.

"If you read the Bible, you will know that the Lord has been portrayed as a jealous disciplinarian. No action of yours will affect God. On the other hand, your actions will determine your destiny.

"The Quran is the only true and final book. Man has altered the Gospel and the Psalms, though they are the Lord's words. After the arrival of the Quran, all other books have lost their value.

"My friend, I will not force you to convert from your religion. But that you will was ordained long ago. If you do convert, know that it is every Muslim's duty to offer Jumma worship five times a day, daily. You may do this alone or in company. Moreover, it is better that you visit the mosque in your place every Friday, to pray.

"In addition, one fortieth of your income must be paid as '*sakkaat*' or 'poor tax'. Apart from this, it is God's bidding that everybody may help the poor according to his financial status."Also, during the ninth month of Ramazan, you should observe a fast for thirty days. On these days, you should not eat anything from sunrise to sunset. There are exceptions to this. The ill, the aged, pregnant women and young children need not observe this fast.

"Finally, it is the duty of every Muslim to go on a holy pilgrimage to Mecca, at least once in his lifetime."

Pausing in his long discourse, Maulana observed Jagan's face, to see his reaction. "What I've said so far, are the basics of Islam. There are some more rules. For example, it is every Muslim's duty to have 'sunnath' performed." Laughing, he looked at Jagan and said, "I have seen you while you bathed. You have already carried out this duty."

"You would have understood from our dietary habits, that every Muslim must eat only food that has been prepared the 'Halaal' way.

"How a Muslim should live, has been taught by the *Hadiths*."

Thus several days passed, learning about Islam from Maulana. "During the 7th century, various forms of idol worship and immorality existed in the Arabian Gulf countries. At that time, it was Mohammed Nabi (sal) who united the Arabs, under the doctrine that Allah was the only God. After this, Islam spread in all directions, from the

Arabian Gulf countries to North Africa, the Middle East, Southern Europe, and Asia. After continuous wars with very strong European kings, culminating in the Crusades, the Ottoman Empire was established. It lasted until the 19ᵗʰ century; it was finally destroyed during World War I. Islam spread to the Eastern regions such as Central Asia, India, and South East Asia, by means of wars as well as commercial links.

"As the land routes from Europe to the Eastern countries were in the hands of the Muslims, the Europeans tried to discover sea routes, and succeeded too in their efforts. Due to this, they not only acquired dominance over the Asian countries, but also propagated Christianity. After the decline of the Ottoman Empire, the Europeans wielded their power in the Middle East also. This condition continues even today.

"Our aim is to out-manoeuvre this, and transform Islam again into a unified force. It is our right to regain what has been captured from us."

After a brief pause, Maulana continued; "We are not racial fanatics; nor are we colour fanatics. We don't enslave others and exploit them. Like the Europeans, we too want to preserve our religious rites without any damage. Whichever race you belong to and whichever language you speak, once you embrace Islam you are my brother".

"What is the position of women in Islam?" asked Jagan hurriedly. "There is a difference of opinion among the Muslims themselves, with respect to the status of women. You'll understand it in course of time," said Maulana.

Under the guidance of Maulana, Jagan learnt to follow the rules of Islam, systematically. He stopped shaving his face. He offered worship like the others, five times a day. Without really understanding, what he was doing and why, he merely followed them and their ways. While in Rome, do as the Romans do says the adage. That was his condition.

However, the Quran and Hadiths, given to him by the Elder, began to change him slowly and gradually. The latter also taught him to understand the Urdu and Hindi languages.

When he thought of his condition - in the midst of a direction-less forest, in a strange house, learning about a different religion and a different language, Jagan felt like laughing. Perhaps this is what Allah has chosen for me, he thought. Moreover, he knew clearly that it was impossible to escape from there, even if he wanted to. And the realization that if he was to fall into the hands of the Indian authorities, he would have to undergo untold misery, made him focus on his present life with renewed enthusiasm.

After a few months, Maulana gave him a newspaper one day. There was an account of the suicides of Sivarasan and Sudha. The Elder told him, "They would have slackened their vigil a little.

I am the Lord

In a few days, I shall take you to a small town. Then you will have the opportunities to learn about the outside world."

The next few days passed in the expectation of a change. As the Greek philosopher Heraclites said, change alone is permanent. This is the rule of the world. If there is no change, man's life will lose its flavour. Not only individuals, even societies and religions keep on changing.

When the Europeans came to India, many Indian women did not wear clothes that covered their breasts. Later, Christian dress codes were imposed, and women accustomed themselves to wear dresses that covered their bodies from head to toe. Today however, things have turned topsy-turvy. Writers like Sigmund Freud and other intellectuals brought about significant changes in European culture. Subsequently, the Western culture underwent a sea change due to the World Wars, the consequent migrations, destruction, and the hippy culture that emerged in the 60s. The computer age and the Internet revolution that followed, transformed the whole world at jet speed. In such circumstances, the lives of individuals are changing every day.

Although it was not idle, Jagan's exiled life did make him feel a little bored.

Hence, when Maulana informed him about their intention to move to a city, a sort of excitement and expectation seized Jagan.

Ezhuth Aani

The next few days passed, with the same expectation and enthusiasm.

Finally, the day arrived. Maulana and his assistants, Amir and Iqbal, asked Jagan to be prepared for the journey. Throughout the night, they walked briskly along paths covered by bushes and canopied by forest trees. They walked for several hours. It may have rained, but they could hear only the rustling of the leaves. As the trees were dense with foliage and closely knit, the raindrops that fell on the ground were very few. The sounds produced by the frogs and other nocturnal creatures were like music played against the background of a basic note – that of the rain.

An eerie darkness so pervaded the forest, that it was immaterial whether it was new moon or full moon, as no light could penetrate the green cover. For the sake of their safety, his friends refrained from talking. To ensure that they did not lose one another, they held on to a long rope. They proceeded along a narrow track like wild ducks in a row.

At last, they reached an open ground, without any trees. Only then, they realized the intensity of the rain. The water there was ankle deep. Many trees had been cut, and a large clearing of land had been cultivated. He did not know then that they were cannabis plants.

When they reached that place, those who were supposed to receive and take them away, had not arrived. Maulana who became alert at this asked them to retreat into the forest and lie low. Only Iqbal was ordered to climb a nearby tree and observe the surroundings. After a few hours' delay, an old van arrived. After checking the occupant's identity, Iqbal summoned the others.

When the van driver saw Maulana, he greeted him, 'Aslamu alaikum'. Maulana returned it with 'Alaikum salaam', and spoke to him in Hindi. Jagan understood some of those words. He learnt that as police patrolling was intense, the driver had to take a detour. As soon as they got in, the van went along a bumpy road full of potholes. Dimming its headlights, the van proceeded very slowly. At dawn, they reached a small Muslim village. The person, who took them there, introduced them as his relatives.

As he had rendered a lot of service to the villagers, they were very loyal to him. Poppy cultivation had yielded him a substantial income. He was generous to the villagers.

After a wash and breakfast, their journey continued by train. They took the Devagiri Express, and after a few hours' travel, reached a small town called Dharmabad. Maulana and his team's support, and their extensive communication network were of great help to the poppy cultivators. At the same time, he spent a major portion of his income on his team and the villagers, in the areas surrounding the forest. Thus, because they led a symbiotic life, they could continue their clandestine trade without the knowledge of the government.

Maulana had arranged that they should stay there for a few months as students in a Madrasa. He told Jagan, "My friend, you will be safe here. Sometime hence, I shall send you elsewhere and out of India." So saying, Maulana took leave of them, to attend to certain affairs related to his organization, which he had not disclosed to them.

From that day, Jagan enjoyed college life once again. Maulana had changed his name to Jamaal. He had embraced Islam more or less fully. Maulana's assistants, Iqbal and Amir were his close companions. That college was exclusively for men. A few months' stay there, gave him a certain fluency in Urdu. He taught his friends English. Though they were not as intimate with him as Maulana was, they continued to be good friends.

# 13

It was 11 p.m. but he could not sleep. He tossed and turned, yet could not find peace. His mother and father, his beloved Olivia, and his sister – their faces kept passing across his mind's screen one after the other. He reflected on the incidents that had taken place after his coming to India. He realized that he had been trapped in a very complex situation. He did not know what the solution to it was. If the same state of affairs continued, he feared that he might never have an opportunity to return to his old life. He cursed himself; he also pitied himself. His thoughts were all dark and sad. He decided to escape from there, and change the course of his life.

The next day, he did not attend college, saying he had a headache. "Brother, will you be able to take care of yourself?" asked Iqbal and Amir worriedly, and left him in the room.

As soon as they left, he got ready. He told the security staff, that he was going shopping. Once out of his sight, he half ran and walked, and reached the station.

He knew that in a few hours' time, they would cast a net for him. The first train to leave that station was the Devagiri Express to Secunderabad. He took a ticket with the money he had taken from the room and sat in a compartment.

He bought a Hindi newspaper and stared at it. Though he did not know to read Hindi, he thought nobody would disturb him if he pretended to be engrossed in reading the paper. After a few hours, the train passed Mirzappalli and was heading towards Secunderabad.

Over and above the clang clang of the train, a voice said, 'Aslamu alaikum'. As he raised his head, a shock awaited him. On both his sides stood hefty men wearing Islamic dresses. Apart from them, there were several others, similarly clad, standing around his seat.

One of them held a small knife against his waist. He had covered his hand with a bag, so that the other passengers could not see the knife.

He then said in Urdu, "If you value your life, come with us."Jagan was very confused. He could not understand whether they were Islamic militants or Indian sleuths in Muslim gear.

Acting on their orders, Jagan detrained at Secunderabad, surrounded by them. He was amused, wondering whether the affluent people and politicians who went around surrounded by security men were just like him, prisoners. Those who enjoy real freedom are the nameless, face-less ordinary people. In the west, the computer age was in the making. It was a time, when it was predicted that everybody could communicate with everybody else with ease. However, one could not help thinking that as communication increased,

I am the Lord

individual liberties would shrink, and finally disappear. In his novel, '1984', George Orwell had predicted forty-two years earlier, that a time would come when governments would spy on their citizens.

As these thoughts passed through Jagan's mind, his captors ordered him to get into an auto rickshaw. He obeyed and sat between them. The auto went zigzag through several streets and lanes, and stopped in front of a huge house. High walls enclosed it. In addition, the garden was full of trees, making the place appear like a fortress surrounded by a moat.

His captors spoke in Urdu. They locked him up in a room and went out. One of them told him, 'Don't try to escape. Otherwise, we shall tie up your hands and legs'.

The window in his room was closed and nailed. Hence, he had to spend his time in darkness! There was a mat and a pillow on the floor. A pot of water and a mug were also there.

He reflected. This was much better than Gupta's prison. He understood too, how foolish he had been to think of escaping from them.

As he analysed the circumstances, one thing became clear. That is, they feared that if they allowed him to escape, it would be dangerous for them; hence, they had locked him up thus. If he roamed around freely, the Indian police would seize him easily. Subsequently, they would torture him and obtain all the details about his friends. Only when he thought of this, the reality struck him that it would mean danger for all of them.

Thus, he realized quite clearly, that for some time, his being with them was beneficial for both. His captors might take him along with them or murder him. However, they would never permit him to go out alone; this was very, very clear to him.

He worried himself, thinking of his stupidity, and how he had lost their trust by his action. Slowly, he fell asleep.

He had no idea how long he slept. Hearing the sound of the door being opened, he woke up. He then heard a familiar voice. Yes. It was Maulana himself. Asking affectionately, "Jamaal, are you still sleeping?" he entered the room.

He then took Jagan to a brightly lit room. Only then, he knew that it was nighttime.

"Jamaal, what you have done is the most foolish thing – betrayal. Have you ever thought of what your condition would have been, if only I had not intervened?"

"In our organization, the punishment for betrayal is death. Your captors would have given it to you as a reward. It was because I requested them to give you another chance, that you are still alive,"

I am the Lord

he said, in the tone of one having the right to chastise.

"Some of the men here feel that bringing you from the prison has been a burden on us. However, I know that you are good. At least hereafter, try not to belie my faith in you.

"I have not forgotten my assurance to you, that I'll help you to leave this country. I was on my way back, to take you to Bombay. By then, you lost your patience. You must be patient."

"Have your meal and sleep. We have to leave early in the morning tomorrow," he concluded lovingly.

Jagan then ate what he was given, finished his prayers and other duties, and went to sleep in his room. This time, his door was not locked from outside. But he knew only too well, that he could not escape.

# 14

The next morning, Jagan woke up early and completed his ablutions, prayers and so on, freely. They took him again to Dharmabad. Iqbal, Amir, and a few other youths were always with him. They looked at him as if he were a worm. Though he knew that they did not trust him, he was not in a position to ask them about it. An uneasy silence prevailed between Jagan and the other youths. Were it not for Maulana's control, they would have torn him to pieces, as lions do deer.

After a few weeks had passed thus, once again they began to treat Jagan as a friend.

Short-tempered as they were, they were equally quick to forgive also.

As soon as the earlier conditions returned, they moved with Jagan as freely as before. However, though they had forgiven him, they had not forgotten his betrayal. Someone or the other was always with Jagan.

During these few weeks, Maulana discussed several things with him. He assured Jagan that he would take him out of India, and after that, he could return to his country as he wished, or join their organization and fight to establish a global government under the leadership of an Islamist

Caliphate. "Allah has a plan for you. If you accept it and act accordingly, you will attain a sublime life."

They discussed various subjects. "In the Old Testament, it is believed that the Arabians descended fromIshmail, the first son of Ibrahim. It was an age when people in the Arabian Gulf countries worshipped various false Gods and idols. Then Allah preached the Quran to Mohammed (sal) through Jibreel, a messenger of God. How could a young man, Mohammed, who had never had any schooling, have created a noble and scholarly work all by himself? From this, you should understand. This book was preached by God, not created by Man."

He continued. "We recognize Jesus Christ as God's messenger, but not as God. After Jesus Christ, the Jews destroyed His teachings, just as they crucified Him. Jesus Christ preached selfless, unconditional love. Paul preached a conditional love; i.e., one that could be controlled by the Church. Moreover, it was said that because Adam ate the forbidden fruit, mankind itself became cursed, and hence, every one of us is born a sinner. In addition, a false philosophy was preached, that we can never reach God through our own efforts or good deeds, but only through Jesus can we attain Heaven.

"Christianity helped to unify and prop up the declining Roman Empire, and to continue its dominance over the world for many more centuries.

"Jesus Christ began a revolution to liberate the Jews and others from the dominance of the Jewish religious heads or Pharisees. That revolution did not stop with His Crucifixion. It was only when Paul seized His doctrines and transformed them, that Christ's revolution was completely defeated. Moreover, we do not acknowledge that Jesus Christ died on the Cross. On the other hand, we believe that He went by land to other countries and lived there. In Kashmir, there is a tomb of a saint called Eesha. Many Kashmiris believe even today that it is Christ's tomb. It was through Christianity that the Western Roman Empire, which was falling apart due to the attacks of Barbarians and Visigoths, was able to survive. Similarly, the Eastern Roman Empire managed to hold on for a thousand years more, because Christianity unified the people and held them together.

"Emperor Constantine embraced Christianity in the 4$^{th}$ century A.D. Whether the Romans surrendered to Christianity, or the Christianity surrendered to the Romans, their union had significant effects. Although the military strength of the declining Western Roman Empire had deteriorated, it was able to retain its dominance by means of the strength of the Christian doctrines.

"The various not so civilized people, responsible for the decline of the Roman Empire, later embraced Christianity and became subjected to the politico-religious authority of the Pope in Rome.

I am the Lord

"It was around this time that Islam, the religion preached by Mohammed (sal) began to spread rapidly. Christianity surrendered to Paul, the leader of the very revisionists who were responsible for diluting the strength of the Christian religion. Christianity surrendered in the capital of the very Romans who crucified Jesus Christ.

"It was under these circumstances, that Mohammed (sal) God's next messenger appeared and guided the people along the right path. The religion founded by Paul and institutionalised by Rome, imposed severe restrictions on the people. By means of levying a tax on religion, and 'confession and pardon', the dominance and financial power of the religious heads grew. Similarly, by using religious beliefs as an illusionary measure, a feudal society was established. Thus, landlords and kings benefitted the most. People were taught not to challenge authority.

"The Christian Church kept the people in a state of ignorance. Many scientific truths discovered by Greek and Roman intellectuals, were blacked out. Hence, scientific progress in the Christian world was blocked for nearly a thousand years. But, Mathematics, Astronomy, and Medicine grew very fast in Arabia and India.

"Orthodox Christianity, under the leadership of the Pope, had created an illusion that it was a sin even to think beyond the Church's preachments.

For example, for more than 1500 years, the theories put forward by Greek scientists like Ptolemy, formed the basis for man's understanding of the universe. The ancients, who were highly superstitious, believed that the earth was flat, and the sun and the stars circled the earth. Contrary to this superstition, although the sages had said as early as 300 B.C., that the earth and the stars circled the sun, orthodox Christianity blacked out such scientific truths. When Copernicus, the Polish astronomer, wrote that the Sun was at the centre of the universe (heliocentric), and that the earth and the other planets went round it, there was strong opposition from the Catholic Church. Later, when scientists like Johannes Kepler modified this theory and Galileo invented the telescope, the Church unleashed its atrocities. Galileo was charged with false accusations, and in his last days, was kept under house arrest. Thus, the Catholic Church succeeded in curbing scientific progress for several centuries. At the same time, the Arab world had already discovered these truths. Take for example, the medical field; the credit for keeping secret for thousands of years, many of the facts which even children know today, goes to the Catholic Church.

"All of us know that with every heartbeat, the blood is pumped through the blood vessels and circulated through the whole body. For more than 1500 years, the Church recognized only the theory of Galen. According to Galen, it was believed that every time the heart beat the blood was spread by diffusion to the various organs. Thus, the Catholic

Church was responsible for the theory that the blood spread from the heart and was absorbed by the organs, and also for not allowing the science of physiology to progress in the Western world, and for letting it stagnate. The Catholic Church, banned the study of man's anatomy (by dissecting the dead body), also proclaimed it a heinous sin. Until the 15th and 16th centuries, when Italy's Leonardo da Vinci and Holland's Andreas Vesalius secretly cut open human cadavers, and discovered that the blood circulates in the body by means of arteries and veins, this truth was not known to the Western world. This too, is an achievement of the Catholic Church. Later, William Harvey demonstrated the circulation of blood in the body; until then the West did not know about it. At the same time, men like Sushrutha in India and Avicenna in the Arab world had already achieved significant success in surgery.

"Until the art of printing reached Europe in the 15th century, the decimal system was not widely followed in the Western world. But, several centuries earlier, this system was followed in India and the Arab world."

Saying thus, Maulana looked at him closely and asked, "Do you know in which language, apart from the European languages, the first book in the world was printed?"

As Jagan remained silent, he continued. "It was in Tamil only. The art of printing, invented by the Chinese, came to Europe in the 15th century.

Ezhuth Aani

Apart from a European language, it was in Tamil that the first book was printed and published. This book described Tamil in Roman letters. Later, Tamil letters were used for books like 'Thambiran Vanakkam'. You should understand one thing. All these books had only one objective – to propagate Christianity among the Tamils."

Citing many examples thus, Maulana said to Jagan, "Do you now understand how Catholicism had an iron hold on men? At the beginning of the 16$^{th}$ century, Renaissance gathered momentum among the intellectuals and artists in Europe. There was a need for reformation. People began to ask questions about the orthodoxy of the traditionalists, and the dictatorship of Catholicism. Western Europe was still under the dominance of the Pope. Questions were raised about that dominance. Due to the rebellion that took place against the Pope, the Christian protestors were called 'Protestants'. It meant 'protestors'. At that time, the English King Henry VIII wanted to divorce his wife, and marry another woman whom he loved. Hence, he established a Church, which did not acknowledge the authority of the Pope. This was the beginning of an independent, autonomous Anglican Church. It is an example of how men modified the Christian religion to serve their ends.

"Because of reformists like Luther and Calvin, that religion has splintered into several groups. You should know that if there are many medicines for, or methods of, curing a disease, none of them

I am the Lord

could ever be said to be better than the others. If it were to be so, everyone would follow only that method of cure. The rest would disappear. Similarly, it is clear from the fact that there are various doctrines and divisions in Christianity, that none of them tells the 'whole' truth. At the same time, the Islamic religion and culture have been a great challenge to the dominance of these people, and continue to be so even now."

Maulana shared his views on various subjects with Jagan. These dialogues were mostly in the form of monologues – Maulana speaking and Jagan listening. One day, contrary to custom, Jagan asked, "May I ask you something?"

"By all means, my friend," said Maulana.

"What is the status of women in Islam?" Feeling guilty that he had perhaps asked a question which he should not have asked, Jagan looked down.

"A good question indeed. Those who follow a kind of Islamic school called 'Vahaabi' or 'Salaafi' practice some of the ancient doctrines blindly. This doctrine originates from Saudi Arabia. Before I explain this to you further, I wish to tell you something very firmly. These theories are not truly Islamic. There are some internal contradictions even within Islam.

"In 1973, though the Gulf Countries were defeated in the Gulf War, this defeat served to unify them. Subsequently, the OPEC, the Organization of the Oil Producing Countries, increased the price of oil manifold. At that time, America played a double game (like making a baby cry and then rocking the cradle) by supporting Israel, and at the same time, looting the world by joining hands with the Arab countries in the oil trade. Seven big oil companies, such as BP, Shell, and Caltex, rule the world in the oil trade. They are referred to as the seven sisters.

"With the new wealth acquired by the rise in the price of oil, the Arab countries became very affluent. Among these, Saudi Arabia used its wealth to help the Muslims in the poor countries. It helped the students with educational scholarships; at the same time, it exported the practice of Vahaabi or Salaafi, which was widely prevalent there. It was these 'salaafis' who were the key founders of Islamic fundamentalism. By means of its financial power, Saudi Arabia propagated this 'fundamentalist' Islam to all corners of the world. It was Saudi's riches that nurtured the war against the Soviet Union, in Afghanistan.

"Under such circumstances, if the other Muslims stood aside and remained mere spectators, the 'salaafis' will gain dominance. Hence, we are duty-bound to involve ourselves with commitment, as brethren."

He continued; "After America was driven out of Iran by the Islamic revolution, in 1979 it offered money and arms to Saddam Hussein, instigating

I am the Lord

him to fight against Iran. From the time of the death of the Prophet, followers of Imam Ali, his son-in-law, have followed the sect called Shia as opposed to the mainstream Sunni faction. The majority of the Islamic world is Sunni. Iran and Iraq are the major Shia majority countries in the world. Though Iraq is a Shia majority country, the ruling elite and Saddam Hussain are Sunni Muslims. Because of America's manipulations, the world's main Shia Muslim countries of Iran and Iraq clashed with each other. Why did America not realize that one day, Saddam Hussein, who was a Sunni Muslim, would turn against America?

"At the same time, America joined hands with Saudi Arabia, and helped Afghanistan rebels to fight against the Soviet Union, by offering them funds and ammunition. As many of the countries that formed part of the Soviet Union also demanded autonomy, the Union disintegrated into many states.

"In the cultural war that is now going on between Islam and Christianity, America is our first enemy. A time will come when we will have to fight against America. Before that, we should fight to strengthen the hands of the reformists of the Islamic world.

"With America's support and Saudi's financial power, it is the 'salaafis' who have gained political and military strength in the Muslim world. This condition will soon change. We are loyalists of the progressive leader, Ahmed Shah Masood.

However, the international community is making strategic moves in Afghanistan. Through the intervention of leaders like Hekmatyar, countries like Pakistan and Iran are interfering in Afghanistan, to safeguard their own interests in the region. Moreover, America's dominance can be seen in countries like Saudi Arabia and Uzbekistan, which also exert influence in Afghanistan.

"But, in our struggle, many Islamic youths have joined us, irrespective of their motherland. Osama Bin Laden from Yemen, Al Zavahiri from Egypt, and Muslims from Somalia, Nigeria, Indonesia, India and several other countries are going to Afghanistan.

"Why, even a non-Muslim from the Western world like you, has joined us because of the will of God.

"In Islam, there are no regional differences; and no caste differences. Many Kashmiri brothers have joined us. Their immediate goal is to liberate Kashmir. Even among these, one group wants Kashmir to be a state of Pakistan. Another group wants Kashmir to be an independent country. The Muslim dominance that existed from the time of Babar to that of Aurangezeb will be re-established in the Indian sub-continent. The Indian government is its first enemy.

"But for men like me, our goal is a global jihad, not just regional interests. Once again, the whole world will be brought under the Caliph's rule, as of old. The main obstacle in achieving this aim of ours is America. If America falls, the Western World will fall. If the Western World falls, the whole world will be at our feet.

"In our journey, no one is a permanent friend. Politics is like travel friendship. For the time being, considering its regional welfare, China is helping us. Very soon, in parts of the Chinese Republic in Central Asia, an Islamic rebellion will break out.

"Even the leaders of countries like Pakistan which is helping us, will soon be thrown out. After our revolution, these corrupt leaders will be wiped out from the face of the earth. There will be no boundaries between countries.

"This is my dream. It may take many years for it to be fulfilled. In the Islamic empire that will be born, the only way to prevent the dominance of regressive traditionalists, who believe in the suppression of women, is for people like us to be united in our struggle and lead it in the right direction."

So saying, Maulana embraced Jagan very warmly. "My friend, we were born in different places in the world, but today we have become brothers, by the grace of God. Our path will henceforth be the same. Our goal and thoughts must travel in the same direction. We shall march ahead in unison. Insha Allah; May success crown our efforts."

After this, they interacted with great mutual understanding. Soon, it was time to leave Dharmabad.

# 15

Dadang, dadang – the sound of the train seemed to reflect Jagan's game of life. Jagan sat at the window, with Maulana next to him and the others next to Maulana.

The newspapers were full of the news about Sivarasan and the police's hunt for him – column after column. Maulana had given Jagan the English daily, The Hindustan Times. The train was running past lush green fields, rocky forests, crossing in between small streams with bridges that lay across them, villages floored with red sand and slums full of tiny huts – like the Goddess of Time. Like Time, the train too did not wait for anybody.

Tired, because of his journey since the afternoon, Jagan went to sleep early. He also woke up early, and looked at his watch. It was four in the morning. The train had stopped at a station.

The sun appeared to be struggling to make the sky pinkish red, in order to liberate the earth from the vicious grip of the dark night.

Perhaps it was customary for the train to stop there for a long time. Some of the passengers had got down to have coffee and breakfast, and were returning. Some others were engaged in their morning ablutions by the trackside. The majority of them were fast asleep, without a care in the world.

There was an electric bulb flickering in the compartment, dimmer than the sunlight outside. He did not notice initially, the young boys who passed by selling newspapers and eats. When one of them crossed him, something prompted Jagan to look back at him. He stared at the boy keenly. On the front page of the newspaper in the boy's hand, was the picture of Maulana himself, smiling! Jagan got up with a start, and bought that Hindi daily. Simultaneously, he shook Maulana awake. Just as the Elder woke up rubbing his eyes, the train began to move, sounding its horn.

Before Jagan could explain the matter to Maulana who was angry at being disturbed from his sleep, the train was hurtling at full speed, tearing through the silent darkness.

As soon as he understood the situation, Maulana told Jagan to keep quiet, and taking his suitcase, he went into the toilet and bolted it from inside.

Just then, the Indian police entered, checking every compartment in the moving train. With Maulana's picture in their hands, they looked at everyone's face. Jagan pretended to read the newspaper, and sat with his heart in his mouth. His previous experience appeared like a shadow before his eyes. He recollected Gupta and his atrocities. For a fraction of a second, he wondered

I am the Lord

if he could escape by confessing the truth, if he were to be caught. The next second, he reprimanded himself. 'What depravity is this? Come what may, I shall not betray my friend' he resolved.

With every second seeming, an age, the police moved on, examining each passenger in the fading darkness, flashing a torch light on his face. Fortunately, they did not have photographs of Jagan and Maulana's associates.

Moving ahead, the police tried to open the door of the toilet, which Maulana occupied. Realizing that it was locked from inside, they banged hard on the door. After two minutes, the sound of the door being opened was heard. 'It's all over' thought Jagan, and turned his eyes towards the door.

Almost hitting the police in the face, the door was opened fully, and a purdah-clad lady stood there. Her clothes, which covered her whole body, could not control her voice. Furious at not being allowed to complete her morning ablutions, she shouted at the police in a squeaky voice, and asked, "What do you want?"

For a second, Jagan wondered if it could be Maulana; but as soon as he heard the voice, he said to himself, 'No, no; this is really a lady'.

Then, where did Maulana go? Did he jump out through the window? Jagan was totally flummoxed. If Maulana had jumped out from a train running so fast, there was no chance of his being alive.

Just then, one of the policemen attempted to lift the purdah, and see the woman's face.

That was the end! The woman transformed herself into Kali, Fury personified. She slapped the policeman on his cheek, and saying 'Ya, Allah', she began ranting in Hindi.

As though they had been waiting for this signal, Maulana's friends Amir and the others started attacking the policeman, chanting Islamic verses.

In a compartment where most of the passengers were Muslims, it was quite easy to stir up pro-Islamic feelings. All of them got together and began to attack those whom they identified as Hindus, including the policemen. Maulana's friends attacked the others, shielding Jagan throughout.

Around this time, someone ran into the neighbouring compartment, and gave the news; thus, the rioting engulfed the whole train. The Muslims believed that one of the policemen tried to molest a Muslim woman, and the Hindus were given to understand that the Muslims had killed a Hindu policeman.

I am the Lord

Amidst this confusion, somebody pulled the emergency chain. With a screech and the sound of metal grating metal, the train came to a halt.

That very moment, the Muslim woman and Jagan's Islamic friends ran into the forest. On their way, they dragged Jagan along with them. By this time, the neighbouring villagers also joined the fray. Asians have been accustomed to view government property as their enemy, whenever they wished to vent their anger against anybody. This train was no exception. Soon, someone set fire to the train, and it began to change into a molten skeleton. Inside, several people too became skeletons.

The group that took Jagan traversed the forest for many hours, walking and running alternately. One of them, having a compass, led the way. The lady had discarded her clothes and stood in a pair of shorts. Yes, it was a clean-shaven Maulana himself.

Jagan asked, "Why are you taking me also?"

"My friend, not knowing their language, if you remain here alone, both sides will kill you. In case you happen to escape, only an Indian jail awaits you. Knowingly or otherwise, I've promised to help you to leave India. I shall fulfil that somehow," replied Maulana calmly.

Then, lost in other thoughts, he said, "You could have betrayed me in the train if you wanted to. You didn't do that. Hence, my respect and regard for you has increased manifold."

I am the Lord

# 16

Traversing through forests and mountainous terrains for several days, it appeared to Jagan that Maulana's group had a network of followers throughout Gujarat. Their time was spent staying in various Muslim villages during the day and travelling during the night. The rioting in the train had taken place near Lonawala, in the Western Ghats. Hence, giving up his plan of going to Bombay, Maulana proceeded towards a town called Vapi, with the help of his network in Gujarat.

Along a path that took them through mountain ranges, rivers and forests, they went East avoiding Bombay, and then North and finally West towards Vapi.

It was a time when the Hindus had begun to clamour for the demolition of the Babri Masjid. Because of this, the Muslims felt that they were alienated in their own country. Although fundamentalism had not spread among the Muslims in the villages, they followed the policy of Muslim brotherhood, and welcomed and hosted any Muslims who passed through their village.

The members of Maulana's group disguised themselves as cloth merchants. Except for a few friends who lived along their route, no one else knew the truth about them.

They shaved themselves clean, wore Western clothes and sarongs, and travelled. They did not, however, give up their practice of praying five times a day.

As their friends had arranged for their cloth bundles, they were able to pass off as merchants from Surat.

Every day, the papers were full of exciting news about how the police conducted their search for Sivarasan, and how they tightened the noose round his neck.

Reports regarding the search for Maulana decreased gradually. The newspapers claimed that Maulana was a bigwig in the Lashkar organization, but when he was arrested and imprisoned, the Indian police did not know his true identity, and hence, were unaware of his importance. Later, when he escaped, the police managed to nab one of his men, and only after he was tortured, did they know Maulana's importance. Subsequently, a search for him was launched on a national scale, and it was then that they came across him suddenly on the train. What should have taken away the head, took only the turban, as the saying goes and Maulana had a narrow shave. Jagan was astonished at Maulana's extraordinary ability to escape, using such tricks as disguise and change of voice.

More than a hundred people, including Muslims, Hindus and policemen, were killed in the rioting on the train. Many bodies were charred beyond recognition. Assuming that Maulana too might have been killed in this incident, the police, in course of time, reduced their search operations. As the whole nation's attention was focused on Sivarasan's accomplices, men who were more dangerous than them were able to escape the scrutiny of the police.

Men like Abdullah Azzaam and Zaafar Iqbal, in Afghanistan, started the Lashkar organization in 1990.

Their ultimate aim was to launch a global Islamic agitation. But their immediate goal was to liberate Kashmir, and destroy countries like India and Israel. Their headquarters was near Lahore. Members of the Lashkar organization maintained close links with the Intelligence Wing of the Pakistan army.

Among the leaders of this organization, Maulana was a progressive thinker. Although they were all fanatic about the Islamic jihad, Maulana also advocated women's liberation. Despite the others, having contrary views, his extraordinary personality, commitment, and sharp intellect won him their respect. He also maintained ties with the Afghan Mujahideen leaders. Ahmed Shah Masood was a great friend of Maulana.

Maulana was arrested when he was engaged in improving the infrastructure of his organization. Although he was known to be an Islamic jihadi, the

Indian Police confined him in an ordinary prison, along with other common offenders, not aware of the full dimension of his status. Very soon, the other Muslim prisoners began to treat him with great respect. Corrupt officers like Gupta also treated him with respect, wishing to avoid any confrontation. The rest of the prisoners had a kind of fear and respect for those who were within the circle of Maulana's patronage. They kept their menacing tendencies to themselves. One or two, who attempted to transgress, soon learnt their lesson. That is, they died in the prison itself. There were several cuts and stab wounds on their bodies. After a few such incidents, Maulana lorded over the prisoners in his own way. It was an unwritten rule, that non-interference was the best policy in matters concerning Maulana. The group that somehow reached Vapi, remained there for some days.

During this period, it became customary for Maulana to go out often during the day and return in the night. Though Jagan was provided with all the basic facilities, the others did not talk to him about any other matter.

One day, suddenly, Maulana brought some saffron dresses. Ten of their group wore those full-length dresses. They got into an old van, travelled for about an hour, and reached a place called Nargol. Maulana said, "This is where Osho alias Rajneesh's meditation centre is located. For the next few days, an event is going to take place here. We shall act as Osho devotees, and merge with the

I am the Lord

others who will be coming from all over the world. After that, I shall inform you of the means by which we can escape from here. You should behave in such a way that nobody suspects us. You need to do what other Osho devotees do. But if any drugs are offered, don't take them." It was his order.

There were many reasons why Maulana chose Nargol. It was not only near the border of Maharashtra and Gujarat, but also close to the Union Territories of Daman and Diu. As all these police divisions overlapped, their vigilance was not strong enough.

Acharya Rajneesh, who changed his name to Osho, must have established his meditation centre in this place, because of its strategic location, thought Jagan.

Osho was an Indian guru. Just as Western religious heads came to India, Indian religious leaders also went west.

Swami Vivekananda, who lived in this world only for 39 years, left his indelible footprint by placing Hinduism and Indian culture in the international arena. In his 30th year, at the Parliament of Religions held in Chicago, USA, he mesmerized the Americans by speaking very eloquently about Hinduism in English.

America, which had achieved remarkable progress economically, had not matched it spiritually. Hence, in the 19th century, to satisfy the

Americans' thirst for spirituality, several new Christian movements appeared. Jehovah's Witnesses, Seventh Day Adventists, Assemblies of God, Pentecostal, and Mormon religion were some of the new sub-divisions that were started in America and England, in the 19th and the beginning of the 20th centuries. Around this time, the Eastern religions too planted their feet in the Western World, and began to propagate their doctrines.

The novel phenomenon of the religions of the colonized countries being exported to the ones that ruled them occurred about this time. This export continues even today.

As far as Hinduism is concerned, after Vivekananda's historic visit, many ashrams were set up in America, which rendered good spiritual service to the Americans. Later, when technologists, doctors, and scientists migrated to the States and the West, they took their religion and the religious heads along with them. Followers of leaders like Sai Baba and Chinmayananda not only spread their preachments in the West, but also drew many Westerners into their fold.

During the two consecutive World Wars that occurred in the 20th century, the youth belonging to the imperialist countries were killed in large numbers. At the end of the World Wars, empires began to decline. For rebuilding the nation, manpower from the Asian and African countries became necessary. Moreover, newly freed countries

I am the Lord

like Kenya and Uganda, tried to evict the Indians who had been planted there by the British. Many of these Indians migrated to England. Thus, due to various reasons, the British Empire over which the sun never set, finally met its doom. That is, there was an age, when it was daytime in some country or the other under British rule. That condition so changed, that the peoples who were in the colonized countries returned to Britain transforming it into a microcosm of the empire it had been earlier. Was this a tangible proof of Isaac Newton's law that, 'For every action there is an equal and opposite reaction?' Had the British not gone to other countries and colonized them, it would not have become a Superpower. Had it not become a Superpower, its art and culture would have been pure and unalloyed. Other cultures or migrants from other countries would not have affected it.

The most important of the migrants to the West were the Indians. Described as a valuable gem in the British crown, Indian culture has taken deep roots in Britain. The Indo-British relationship can be described as a man-woman relationship. Just as a man captures a woman and makes her his own, Britain had captured India and kept it as a slave under its control. The woman, silently and slowly overwhelms the man, and transforms him totally. Similarly, Indian traditions and culture have taken a hold on the British, and changed their society completely. Indian curries, perfumes, art, and culture have become an indispensable part of British life.

Apart from this, earlier, the British used to take raw materials like cotton from India, make clothes out of it, bring them back to India, and sell them here. Many Indians were taken to Britain to work in the textile mills there. These mills were the result of the Industrial revolution that took place in the 18th and 19th centuries. To counter this, Mahatma Gandhi had begun the Khadi movement. However, two centuries later, with the advent of various synthetic materials, the textile industry has moved from the West to the Asian and African continents. But the descendants of the workers who had been taken from the Indian sub-continent to work in the mills in Britain, settled in the midlands there. Because of the unemployment and poverty prevailing amidst them, they were attracted by religious fundamentalism.

Whatever it may be, the hippy culture of the 60s may be considered as a highpoint of India's cultural impact on the West. Members of this movement appeared to be alienated from the mainstream politics of the Western World, and to favour equality and peace. They had combined Eastern religions, music etc., with Western culture. They came to be identified with the permissiveness associated with drug addiction, free sex and so on. They also opposed the Vietnam War, politically.

It was against this background that Bhagwan Rajneesh's impact spread through the world.

Born Chandramohan Jain, he changed his name to Acharya alias Bhagwan Rajneesh. He set up an ashram in Pune in 1974. Many Western

I am the Lord

devotees, both male and female, came in search of him. His teachings on sex made him a controversial figure. In the 80s, because of the opposition from the Indian government and the Indian neighbours, he migrated to the state of Oregon in America. He and his devotees set up a place called Rajneeshpur and settled there. Controversies dogged him there also. In the midst of various criminal allegations concerning drug trafficking, possession of fire arms and so on, he left America, and visited several countries in some of which he felt unwanted, and finally, returned to India itself. Changing his name to Osho during his last days, he died in 1990. However, his policies and doctrines continue to live even today. It was under these circumstances, that the Conference organized by the Osho Foundation, in which Maulana and Jagan participated, took place.

Nargol, which was brimming over with devotees from many countries, appeared like a sea of red poppy flowers. A house had been allotted to Maulana's group. The members went out in different directions during the day, and returned home only at night. Jagan, who had practically no work to do, spent his time exploring the surroundings of Nargol, learning its history, and now and then participating in the dances of the Osho group. Maulana had given him strict orders on certain things; offer worship five times a day without being seen by anybody; do not talk much to strangers; and avoid women and drugs. He was given full freedom, otherwise. Nevertheless, one of his group members was with him most of the time.

Hence, the thought of violating Maulana's orders never occurred to him.

Nargol, a small village, was of historical importance. When the Muslims captured the Persian Peninsula in the 10$^{th}$ century B.C, the Zoroastrians who originated from Iran, wishing to escape from the aggressors, took the sea route and landed in India; Nargol was the place where they first set their feet on. For nearly 200 years, they had fought against the Muslims, and met only with defeat. Most of them embraced Islam. The rest, who could not reconcile themselves to this conversion, took refuge in India. Though they settled in Nargol, they gradually began to move to Bombay. However, a 'Fire Temple' built by the Parsis, remains in Nargol even today. When Jagan went to see that temple, he was introduced to a man. Calling himself Billimoria, he explained his religion to Jagan.

According to their belief, there was only one God. His name was Ahura Mazda. He created this world. Through His messenger, Zoroaster, He let mankind know the Truth. His teachings have been collected and presented in the sacred book called 'Avestha'. Zoroastrianism is chronologically older than Judaism, Christianity, and Islam. Zoroastrianism first advocated the principle of one God. It is believed that some of the basic tenets of the religions that appeared later were inspired by the religion of Ahura Mazda. They believe that there was a war between the Good and the Evil. They believe that Ahura Mazda is fighting against

I am the Lord

one equal to Satan, called Angra Mainyu, and finally, when Mazda wins heaven will be established on earth. They also believe that one can cleanse oneself only by following the three basic policies of good thoughts, good words, and good deeds. They offer worship several times a day.

"Being followers of Ahimsa (non-violence), our religion has had an impact on all the religions descended from Abraham. But, as we do not involve ourselves in violence like them, we have not tried to propagate our religion," said Billimoria.

Jagan repeated what Billimoria had said, to Maulana. He laughed and told him, "You are very confused. You should understand one thing. The Parsis and their Zoroastrian religion are both declining in the world. What is the reason for this? People have rejected their philosophy. Do not burden your mind with such thoughts hereafter. Tomorrow, Rajneesh's devotees may tell you something else. You should learn to take these things in one ear and let them out through the other." Maulana laughed again.

# 17

The beauty of Nargol attracted Jagan. Its white sandy beaches, the casuarina groves adjacent to the beaches and the coconut palms that peeped through the casuarina trees were all very beautiful.

The seawater was white with foam and sand. He learnt that there were many sea turtles in the Arabian Sea. There were some boats and fishing gear on the seashore.

There were many rumours that in this area called Cambay Bay lay Dwaraka, once Lord Krishna's capital. Fishermen, who dared to go deep into the sea to retrieve their nets, reported having seen remnants of a city in the form of temple tops and walls. Despite these rumours, the Archaeological Department of India did not show much interest in that place.

Two days later, Maulana woke up Jagan at midnight. "Come with me. Shouldn't ask any question," he said. After walking along a narrow path in the casuarina grove for half an hour, they reached a dense forest-like area. There were trees right up to the sea. It was the estuary of a small river. The water level there would change often. The salinity of the water would also change according to the tide. The trees too, had adapted themselves to such an environment. Some of the roots had grown above the water level and were sharp as needles. If one were to tread on those roots, it would be like climbing up a stake. 'Be careful' said Maulana. Then, asking him to wait, he disappeared. In the pitch darkness, he could hear various sounds made by different animals and creatures. Jagan stood there, terrified. When he wondered if crocodiles could come there, his fear increased. As crocodiles were capable of leaping a distance of several feet, Jagan felt it would be difficult to escape from them.

After some time, he could hear men speaking. There were two of them. One was Maulana. The other's voice was not familiar. When they came close, Maulana signalled to Jagan with the help of a small light, to come closer. He obeyed. Talking to the stranger in Marathi or Gujarati, a language that he could not understand, Maulana turned to Jagan and said to him in English, "I have told him that you are a Rajneesh devotee from Greece. I have told him that you are a millionaire merchant and that you are crazy about drugs. Act accordingly. I shall take care of the rest."

The fairness of Jagan's complexion, his dark hair, and other facial features could make people believe easily that he was a Greek. When he was in school, his Greek friends treated him very cordially, because he was similar to them in appearance. Why, even his girlfriend Olivia, was of Greek origin. Jagan was astonished at Maulana's sharp intellect and his ability to assess any situation or matter, in a trice.

The stranger treated Jagan with great respect. He took them to his boathouse. It was so sheltered by the casuarina trees, that it was not visible from the outside. As the waves here were rather strong, very few regular fishermen visited the place.

The three of them got into waist-deep water and reached a boat tied to a tree in the middle of the sea. Only when the tide was high during the nights, will the sea here be deep enough for a boat to enter. At other times, when the sea retreated, the place will have sand and bushes, with small trees here and there. Then, these boats would be kept hidden in the casuarina groves.

"Walk carefully; follow our footsteps; if you put your feet on the sedges, you'll be hurt," said Maulana in English.

After the two of them got into the boat, the stranger untied it, pushed it into the sea for a few feet, and then got in. With the help of the two oars in the boat, he steered it into the deep sea. After about two hours' travel thus, a huge fishing trawler came into their view. Anchored in the middle of the sea, the ship had the Indian flag flying at its mast.

As the boat neared the ship, suddenly, people could be seen moving on the deck above. After ascertaining the identity of the boatman by means of light signals, they allowed the boat to come closer. As the boat tossed about in the sea waves, a rope ladder was lowered from the ship. The 40 feet long fishing trawler had two decks. The upper deck had the engine room and two other rooms. The lower one contained various bundles and sacks, fishing equipment, a refrigeration room and so on.

When they reached the upper deck, two big figures screened them. Then, they took them to the room next to the engine room. Those who took them, made them sit there, and went out. When the two of them looked around the room, they noticed that there were very few items of furniture – a small cot, a table and four chairs. That was all. To save electricity and to avoid attracting other boats, only a few bulbs provided a little light to the ship.

Shortly, the ship's captain arrived. A native of Maharashtra, he spoke a few words to them, and confirmed that they were indeed traders. He then spoke to Jagan in broken English. Maulana had introduced Jagan as Pappas. Jagan informed him that he was a drug trafficker, and that he supplied drugs not only to members of Rajneesh's group, but also to his regular customers in India and Sri Lanka. He said that his headquarters was in Colombo, and that he visited Bombay often. Other details could be discussed with his manager, said Jagan, and fell silent.

Maulana said that his name was Raj, that he belonged to Haryana, and then spoke about things in general for some time. They then discussed their trade dealings.

After about half an hour's conversation, Maulana and the captain of the ship appeared to be long-standing friends. Saying that he would return, Maulana bid him farewell. Once again, the boat journey continued in silence. During the next few days, Maulana and Jagan went to the ship every night, and interacted with the crew. The ship's captain was merely a small time trader. He brought small quantities of drugs from Afghanistan. At other times, he carried on fishing in earnest. On specified days, the goods (contraband) would arrive in Pakistani boats. These goods would change hands in the middle of the sea. As the captain's confidence in these people grew, he began to confide in them his personal details. He was an alcoholic. Knowing this, Maulana had gifted him some foreign varieties of liquor. Although Maulana did not drink liquor, he gave the captain company, by taking fruit juices. He allowed Jagan to drink occasionally, but not more than one or two pegs. He feared that if the youth became intoxicated, he would blurt out the truth. But he also knew that if a Greek man refused liquor, it might arouse suspicion.

The next few days passed in this manner. During the day, the ship moved further into the sea, pretended to be engaged in fishing, returned to the same place at night and cast anchor. Maulana and his group knew that during the smuggling operation, there would be only five men in the ship including the captain; during regular fishing activity, there would be some others also. Only the five-crew members knew about the smuggling.

I am the Lord

They realized that if more men knew about it, their secret would no longer be a secret.

Maulana's group learnt that the basement of the ship contained AK 47 rifles, carefully kept hidden. Apart from this, a pistol was kept in the captain's table drawer. When the captain showed it proudly to Maulana, the latter had secretly removed the bullets.

During the next few days, Maulana introduced five of his group members to the captain. Anticipating that the smuggling that had been carried on now and then on a small scale would henceforth become a big business, the captain became very happy. The advance amount, the liquor bottles and a small radio set which Maulana gave him, increased his joy and expectations manifold.

While the nights passed thus, Jagan spent the daytime in dancing with the Rajneesh group members, and exploring the places around.

At this time, he came across the 'Nirmaal' tree, a kind of casuarinas tree. He also met Billimoria there. The latter told him, "The Abrahamic religions have integrated our beliefs into their religion." Though Jagan knew some of these things, he kept silent.

"The Last War, the Last Judgment and so on are our tenets. Some of the views propounded by our religion have been mentioned in the Bible and

Quran also. At the end, everyone will rise from the grave. A Saviour will come; he would have been born out of Immaculate Conception; such beliefs are there in our religion. Some of Abrahamic religions claim that every man's destiny has been pre-ordained by God. We do not believe in this. That is, we believe that every man has the freedom to act according to his will.

At the Last Judgment, whether he goes to heaven or hell will depend on his deeds. Moreover, according to our belief, hell is not permanent. The souls that go to hell can redeem themselves by performing acts of remediation." He paused and asked Jagan, "Do you know the significance of this tree?"

"No," said Jagan. "The Movement called Sagajayoga, founded by Matha Nirmala Devi teaches us how meditation awakens the Kundalini energy, and how through this we can understand ourselves. It was in May 1970, when Mataji was meditating under this tree called Nirmaal tree, that the last *chakra,* namely, the *Sahasraara chakra* in the brain was awakened. History has recorded that it was after the awakening of this seventh chakra, that she acquired the Kundalini energy.

"Those who practice Sagajayoga belong to various religions. The ancient religious treatises say that the Kundalini energy can be awakened only by practicing yoga, and following the path to Salvation. The Sagajayogis believe that the

I am the Lord

Kundalini energy can be acquired through meditation and Mathaji's presence.

"According to Sagajayoga, there is another body apart from our material human body. It is made of Chakras and the nerves that connect them. Scientists are realizing this gradually. The Sympathetic Nervous System and the Parasympathetic Nervous System are considered to be the ida, pingala, and sukshmana nerves. By awakening the Kundalini energy that lies static at the lower part of our spinal cord, we can harness the energies lying in the various chakras. By means of this, we can cure diseases. Once we elevate ourselves thus, we can attain Salvation. This is their philosophy.

"When Nirmala Devi was born, she was called Nirmala Srivatsava. During her spiritual quest, she met several gurus, including Rajneesh. Learning that he was fooling the people, she found what she was searching for, through her own meditation. Her followers consider her as the incarnation of Goddess Shakthi Herself. It is this Primordial Shakthi, which the Christians call the Holy Spirit.

"It is said that those who follow Sagajayoga are in a state of permanent bliss. They call it a state of Realisation devoid of thoughts. Those who have experienced it, claim that it brought about several changes in their lives. Nirmala Devi has imposed many restrictions in the dietary habits of her devotees.

"There are people who consider her as the incarnation of the Goddess, and perform poojas to her. Mataji says that by performing poojas, we can become one with the cosmic energy present in the universe.

"However, there are also allegations that she interferes with the personal lives of her devotees. Right from the choice of who could marry who to various personal decisions, the devotees of Mataji were expected to obtain her permission. Those who wished to break free from such control were expelled from the organization."

Billimoria continued; "People are in a spiritual vacuum. There are several religious heads who want to exploit people's weaknesses. Each person should analyse things independently and then decide. Once you surrender your mind to somebody, you will lose your freedom and free thinking power completely." He then took leave of Jagan.

# 18

That day also dawned. When they came to Nargol, Jagan knew that Maulana arrived there only with some plan. Then, when they undertook secret nocturnal trips, Jagan had great expectations that something was about to happen by sea. On one hand, he was excited that they were going to leave India; on the other, an unknown fear as to what would happen next, subjected him to experience two very different emotions simultaneously.

It was a new moon day. Most of the devotees of Rajneesh who came to Nargol, had left in different directions, and only a few remained. Maulana, who bought the boat, asked the boatman to go to Bombay, stay there for a week and then return. The boatman knew that some smuggling activity was going on; but as he was given enough money, he left for Bombay to see his wife and children. With the money that Maulana gave him, he could buy two boats.

Apart from Maulana and Jagan, five more men got into the boat. Rowing hard, they reached the mid-sea. As it was new moon, it was pitch dark everywhere. A fog restricted the visibility further. The sea was silent. Jagan wondered if the calm was before or after the storm.

As the sea was silent, the 'cluck, cluck' sound of the oars pushing the water, was rhythmic. As the boat moved farther and farther from the seashore, the sounds of the nocturnal creatures also decreased, and then stopped altogether.

Once the boat approached the ship, by means of the now-familiar light signals, both sides communicated with each other. Then, when the rope ladder was lowered, they climbed up to the ship one by one. While one man remained in the boat, six of them got into the ship. As they had become familiar, the ship's crew did not subject them to careful scrutiny. They had come today to buy several kilos of drugs, paying a lot of money. From being a petty smuggler, the captain would henceforth be a wholesale merchant; this thought made him very happy.

Maulana and Jagan were discussing with the captain the modalities of the payment of money, and the transfer of goods from the ship to the boat. The others went with the captain's men to the lower deck.

Suddenly, they heard a scream. The captain became alert. He jumped up and took out his gun. "Hands up! Surrender immediately or you'll die," he said.

Maulana laughed aloud. "I removed the bullets from your gun long ago," he said.

I am the Lord

The captain aimed his gun. But, there were no bullets. Suddenly he got up. Before they could move, he took out another gun from his trouser pocket, and not only shot at Maulana twice, but also pressed the distress signal button.

Maulana fell flat on the ground and asked Jagan to do the same. Luckily, the bullets did not strike them. In the meanwhile, Amir who came up shot the captain with his AK 47 rifle with a volley of bullets. Breathing his last, the captain fell to the ground.

Maulana told Amir, "Good thing you came. The fact that we did not know about the captain having a second gun, is a failure of our intelligence work. If only you had not come, our plan would have been blown to pieces."

Amir said, "We slit all their throats and killed them. One of them screamed before we could gag his mouth. The two AK 47 rifles which they had are now with us!"

"The captain has sounded the alarm. We don't have much time. The Indian navy may close in on us any moment. Raise the anchor immediately." Maulana was obviously in a hurry.

The man, who had remained in the boat, left it and got into the ship. Amir took charge of the engine room, while the others began cleaning the trawler. They took the captain's bullet riddled body and threw it into the sea. They then went down to the lower deck. Jagan's blood froze at what he saw there. Was this the darker side of Islam? All religions have an ugly side to them. It is the same with Islam. Four men lay with their throats slit, looking up. Their mouths and eyes were wide open. The blood from their necks had flowed like a river and congealed. The whole place was covered with blood.

Maulana said, "It's not a sin to kill those who are not Muslims. Moreover, we killed them only out of necessity. Their death must have come quickly. Better still, we killed them by the 'halaal' method."

They dragged their bodies and threw them into the sea.

"After we reach Pakistan, we can clean the ship. Right now, our need is to get out of Indian waters," said Maulana.

With Amir at the steering wheel, the ship's anchor was raised, and it began moving away from the shore.

Just then, Amir shouted, "Sheikh! They're following us."

Far away, two patrol boats could be seen coming towards them.

Their ship's speed could not match that of the patrol boats. The distance between them began to

I am the Lord

decrease. Even after journeying a few hours, they could not reach the Pakistani seas. Maulana asked Amir to give up this plan, and try to reach the international maritime borders. The Indians would not leave them. Soon, those in the boats began to use their guns. In retort, Maulana's group also shot with their AK 47 rifles. The Indians' guns were more powerful than theirs.

Suddenly, a scream 'Allah' was heard. Yes. It was Maulana's voice. He lay on the ground, struck on his chest and abdomen by bullets and shrapnel. In the meanwhile, some of the bullets had pierced the sides of the ship, and slowly the water began to enter the ship.

Whatever their intent, the Indian boats left their chase and returned to the Indian seas.

In Maulana's ship, there was utter confusion. His blood mixed with that already on the deck. Was this, what is referred to as 'blood of my blood?' Maulana appeared pale, drained of his blood, struggling to breathe, and the veins on his neck bulging out.

He ordered Jagan, "If there is a needle and a syringe in the first-aid box in the ship, bring it; and tell Amir to go as fast as he can to the Pakistani maritime border." He also asked him to send a radio message to the Pakistan Naval command control centre. 'Sheikh Omega has been wounded' was the message. They sent a reply saying, 'It will take many hours for us to come to your help'.

Ezhuth Aani

Amir ordered the others to bail out as much water as they could from the ship. They had barely about one and a half hours to save themselves, before the ship sank.

Just then, Jagan entered with the needle. Maulana told him, "A bullet has pierced my heart. Because of the hole caused by the bullet, blood is oozing into the sac surrounding the heart. In this condition, I may die any moment due to the pressure on the big veins. If you do as I say, I may last about half an hour."

"I shall do whatever you say," said Jagan.

Maulana asked him to jab the needle just below the ribs in the middle and move it in the direction of the left shoulder. Jagan hesitated. "There is no time. Already I am in great pain. Don't think you'll pain me any more by this needle."

His eyes began to close. He struggled to breathe. Jagan stabbed with the needle as instructed. Immediately, the blood rushed into the syringe. After about 20 ml of blood had been drained, his breathing eased and his eyes opened again.

Amir and Jagan kneeled near him, greatly worried. The others tried to bail out the water from the ship. Slowly, the ship began to sink.

I am the Lord

When Maulana attempted to raise his head, he felt dizzy. Hence, he lay down again and held both their hands.

"I shall reach God soon. I wish to tell you a few last words. Amir, I know that you do not like Jamaal much. Ever since he ran away from Dharmabad, you have been eyeing him with suspicion. You have tolerated him for my sake. I am worried as to what you'll do to him after I'm gone. You must promise me that you will protect Jamaal as your own brother."

He then looked at Jagan and told him, "I have brought you out of India, as I promised. If you are able to survive until the Pakistani navy arrives, you can go to Pakistan. After that, you can live as you wish. If you dedicate yourself to the service of Allah, He will give you all that you want.

"As soon as you reach Pakistan, you can join the Mujahideen rebels. Try to steer them in a progressive path, away from their regressive doctrine of treating women as slaves. You can join my friend, Ahmed Shah Masood. Some of the Lashkar leaders may oppose this. May you succeed in overcoming these internal contradictions," he said, and closing his eyes, his head dropped.

He stopped breathing. Suddenly, his face became serene. They realized that he had reached a state, away from the pain, breathlessness, dizziness and such physical aches that he had suffered from all this while. When he realized that they had lost their Guiding Spirit, Amir sobbed his heart out. Jagan too cried. He wept with the heavy feeling that he had lost a dear, respected friend or relative to the darkness of death. During the '83 riots, he was worried only about saving himself and his family, and hence, had not understood the severity of the loss of life and property that took place around him. Tonight, he saw for himself many deaths; and now, the reality that one whom he loved dearly had left him forever, stared him in the face, and he could not refrain from crying.

After a few minutes' weeping, Amir got up and embraced Jagan. "My friend, henceforth consider me as your brother. I shall protect you as the eyelid does the eye," he said, in a grief-stricken voice.

Both of them wrapped Maulana's body in a cloth, said a few prayers, and with heavy hearts threw it into the sea.

The next minute, Amir assumed the role of a captain. With two thirds of the ship already under water, he realized that they could remain in the ship only for a few minutes. He therefore ordered all the others to wear the life jackets that were in the captain's room. He then reminded them to take some of the things that would help them to float in the sea. He asked them to take drinking water in whatever plastic bottles they could lay their hands on, and a small radio. He then took a long rope, and tied it round their waists, so that they could remain together.

I am the Lord

"If we sink, all of us will sink. If we survive, all of us will survive. In Allah's name leave the ship," he ordered.

As soon as he felt the seawater on his body, Jagan's hands and legs nearly froze. When the cold water hit his chest, he thought his heart would stop. As they floated in the middle of the sea, Amir said, "We should save our energy. Do not talk and don't try to swim. It is enough if you keep treading water with minimum use of your hands and legs."

There was a distance of nearly ten feet of rope between each of them. It was the rope used to anchor the ship. It had been knotted around each one's waist. As the knot was very tight, Jagan's waist began to be bruised. He tried to move the rope a little up and down, to relieve his pain.

Jagan was tired of watching the stars twinkling. Having engaged himself in trying to count the stars, losing their count, and beginning once again, he felt as if Time stood still.

As it was new moon day, there were not many waves in the sea. Jagan began to reflect on his condition. He had been living a very sheltered and ordered life. Now, here he was with complete strangers, tied to them with a rope, and floating with his life at stake. Wondering how life takes man through sudden twists and turns, to entirely new environments, Jagan began to concentrate on not falling asleep. As they had to shout to make themselves heard above the roar of the sea, they remained silent. Though they were tied together with a rope, they had to spend the night only as islands. To prevent being drowned in the water, they kept splashing their hands and legs. Only if they avoided unnecessary movements, they could be safe until help arrived. In that static condition, lulled by the waves, the Goddess of Sleep was longing to embrace them. To drive away slumber, Jagan smeared his eyes with a little salt water. He found it very difficult to keep away sleep when the body was tired and weak.

Jagan felt as if fishes were swimming between his legs. He wondered if there were sharks in the sea. Nevertheless, he thought there was no point in thinking of dangers until one met them.

Also, if he were to pray to God to save him, he was confused as to which God to pray to. When he was young, during exam time, his mother used to pray to Lord Ganesha. But, since his association with Maulana, he had come to regard Lord Ganesha and Muruga only as stone idols created by man. At the same time, he could not accept an Islamic God wholeheartedly. Hence, he gave up the idea of praying to God to save him.

His hands began to wrinkle because of the salty seawater soaking them. The knot around his waist also began to hurt him badly. As they felt that their clothes absorbing the seawater would increase their weight, they were clad only in their undergarments.

I am the Lord

Lost in thought about his physical discomfort and mental agony, Jagan suddenly felt that something was dragging him down into the sea. His rope was pulled forcefully, and was trying to pull him also into the sea. Must be a whirlpool he thought, and began to swim against the current. Some superior force appeared to drag him deeper. He thought his end had come. His entire life passed before his eyes, like a movie. Twenty years of his life passed in a few seconds. In the presence of birth and death, time loses its meaning. His inner voice told him, 'No use fighting any more. Drink the water and just drown'. Just then, he was released suddenly from the force that had pulled him down. He realized that he was being raised towards the surface of the water. When he came up, he looked close and found that it was Amir who had pulled him up by his rope.

Amir swam towards him. "As some of them dozed off, they were drowned. So, I cut off the rope that tied them. They have all been drowned.

Only the two of us are alive. If I hadn't cut the rope off, all of us would have died. Then there will be no one to take forward Sheikh's dream! If we are able to manage for a few hours more, our friends will certainly come to save us. I have kept the word I gave Sheikh Maulana. We shall somehow escape from this sea. We have a lot of work."

Saying this, Amir advised him to keep floating.

Ezhuth Aani

After some time, the sun slowly rose in the East. The ugliness of the dark night began to give way to the hope of the daytime. The dawn which began as a red streak, soon engulfed the whole sky in red and orange hues. The sun appeared as a golden ball in the East.

As the range of light increased, Jagan began to realize the dimensions of the sea around him. There was water everywhere, with no sign of land. How could they escape from there? In which direction could they swim? Did they have the strength to swim and reach the shore? As he kept asking himself all these questions, Jagan suddenly noticed Amir operating an instrument hanging from his neck. It was a radio. He was informing his friends about their location by means of its signals.

Until sunrise, Jagan longed for sunlight. When the sun rose in all its glory, he wilted in its heat. Similarly, in life too, we long for the friendship of affluent and influential men; then, we wither unable to bear their whims and fancies. As the sun's heat increased, his tongue became parched. His lips went dry. His eyes became red, unable to bear the intense light.

Water, water everywhere, but not a drop to drink! He knew that if he were to drink salt water, he would die sooner.

A few hours passed in this agony. He did not even have the energy to talk to Amir. If death is certain, why prolong it? If he were to cut off the

I am the Lord

rope, he would drown and end his ordeal, he thought.

Just then, far away, a white boat could be seen. Gradually, what was a small dot became bigger. After a few minutes, it came towards them, and then went off in a different direction. After they had experienced hope and disappointment once or twice again, a small boat came fast, this time truly towards them. Amir took a few pieces of red and white cloth floating near him, and waved them. Those in the boat saw them. It was a mechanised dinghy. There were three men in it; all of them were armed. As they came close, they spoke to Amir in Urdu. After asking a few questions, they pulled up both of them into their boat. The first thing they needed on getting into the boat was water.

They did not want food to eat, or clothes to wear. All that both Amir and Jagan wanted was water to drink.

As soon as they got into the boat and drank water, whether he slept or fainted, Jagan did not know. When he opened his eyes, he knew that the boat was approaching a big harbour.

It was Port Quasim, situated at the mouth of the Sind River. Through one of the waterways that surrounded the port, the boat travelled some distance and reached a small boat jetty. There, under the supervision of the naval officers, they were disembarked and taken for interrogation.

Ezhuth Aani

Treating Amir very cordially, they enquired about Maulana's passing away. Then, they were given a banquet. A sumptuous feast was served, including various fruits. Later, a room was allotted to them to rest and sleep.

Before they went to bed, Amir told Jagan, "My friend, this is the beginning of the next stage of our journey."

I am the Lord

# 19

The whole of the next day was spent in travelling. Amir and Jagan journeyed in a jeep from Karachi to Lahore. Nicknamed Pakistan's 'Garden City', Lahore was indeed a beautiful city.

Capital of the Punjab State, Lahore was very close to the Indian border. Perhaps it was due to this fact that many Islamic outfits had set up their bases there. Tradition has it, that one of Lord Rama's sons, Lava, established this city. Even today, there is a temple for Lava there. Now, worship is not offered in the temple. Situated on the banks of the River Ravi, a tributary of the River Sind, there is evidence to prove that Lahore is about 2000 years old. Gazni Mahmud, who defeated the Hindu kings Jayapala and Anandapala who ruled from Kabul, captured Lahore and made it his own.

Lahore city was captured only after a prolonged siege. Hence, it was an army commander called Malik Ayaz, who built a new city on the ruins of old Lahore. In that city, the Lahore fort has been rebuilt and even today, stands tall and majestic, a testimony to an ancient culture.

In the 16th century, King Babar, a descendant of Genghis Khan, invaded India and established the Mogul Empire. It lasted for about 250 years.

During the Mogul rule, Lahore was prosperous and the Lahore fort was expanded and renovated. For a short time in the 18th century, Lahore came under the control of the Marathas, and later became the capital of the Sikhs for some time. Then, Britain captured what is now India, Pakistan, and Afghanistan. In 1947 when the British left, Punjab was divided into two; Amritsar and the other sacred cities of the Sikhs were given to India, while Lahore went to Pakistan.

Many of the Hindus who were indifferent to who ruled them (Rama or Ravana) converted to Islam, while some converted to Sikhism, and some to Christianity. Today they live as different communities, having forgotten that they are all descended from the same forefathers.

Emperor Ranjit Singh had all the lands from the Khyber Pass to Kashmir under his control. After his death, due to the internal squabbles in his family, Sikh dominance declined, and the British took over the reins. During the Indo-Pakistan partition, Punjab broke into two. Many families were caught on both sides of the border and were separated. Several of those on the Pakistani side, who were not Muslims, converted to Islam. At the same time, Kashmir, which had been an independent state, aligned with India. The King of Kashmir was not a Muslim, but most of the citizens were. Hence, Pakistan staked its claim to Kashmir. India and Pakistan fought to capture the land in Kashmir. They shared the lands within the borders of the state of Kashmir. Slowly, China swallowed the North Eastern parts of Kashmir. Aksai Chin, which belonged to India, was captured by China. Though India and Pakistan fought over Kashmir, not much is reported about China's encroachments. Even the fundamentalists in Kashmir now consider India as their enemy, but do not pay much attention to China. India's enemies are trying to forget, for the time being, that China too has intruded into Kashmir.

There are many tombs and big mosques in Lahore. Two of them attracted Jagan. One was Anarkali's and the other, Iqbal's. Salim, the son of Emperor Akbar, who was renowned for his righteousness and sense of justice, fell in love with Anarkali, a slave. Enraged by this, Akbar ordered Anarkali to be entombed alive. This very Salim later became Emperor Jehangir. His elder son, Khusru rebelled against his father. Jehangir suppressed the rebellion, blinded Khusru, and let him live. His second son, Qurram also rebelled against him. Both Khusru and Qurram were born to a Hindu Rajput mother. Qurram subsequently became Emperor Shah Jahan. It was he who built the Taj Mahal, an epic in stone. That he had the hands of the workers who built the Taj cut off later is another tragic story. It is similar to that of Ekalaivan in the Mahabharata. Shah Jahan built the Taj Mahal as a monument of love to his wife. Once again, there was a war between the sons of Shah Jahan for the throne. Aurangazeb, who won, imprisoned Shah Jahan. Thus, their own sons deposed all the Mogul kings. Jagan wondered whether Anarkali's curse was responsible for this.

Allama Iqbal was a poet greatly loved by the Pakistanis. He lived in Lahore. An important member of the All India Muslim League, he was a close friend of Mohammed Ali Jinnah. Even two decades before India's independence, he had made a demand that a Muslim nation must be created in the Indian sub-continent. In the song, 'Sare Jahan Se Acha' written in 1904, Iqbal had praised Hindustan highly. The content of the song was this; 'Bharat is the best country in the world; religion cannot divide us; all of us are Indians, and India is our motherland'. This same Iqbal, after five or six years, wrote another song 'Tharana-e-milli', set to the same tune. In that song he said, 'Central Asia, Arabia, and India, are all ours. We are Muslims. The whole world is our motherland'. This change in Iqbal reflected the religious feelings that were slowly taking shape in the minds of the Muslims. Even today, Pakistan is one of the foremost countries that are nurturing Islamic fundamentalism. Iqbal's lyrics continue to live to this day, in countries like India, Pakistan, and Iran.

Amir and Jagan spent a few days sightseeing Lahore. They then occupied themselves in achieving their goal in earnest.

When Afghanistan was engaged in a war against the Soviet Union, the recruitment of young men for an Islamic war, took place openly in cities like Lahore. Various organizations had their

I am the Lord

communication networks in Pakistani cities. Thus, anybody could join any organization, if he wished. This war was conducted with the help of funds from Saudi Arabia and arms from America, from Pakistani bases.

Jagan and Amir searched for and found the office of the Lashkar movement, and introduced themselves.

First, certain investigations were carried out, and their backgrounds were screened. Then they were enrolled in the training camps. There, they were taught the basic tenets of Islam, along with the art of war.

They were subsequently sent to the camps in the mountain ranges of Baluchistan province.

It was there, that they met Ahmed Shah Masood by chance. At that time, the various organizations helped one another functionally. Members of the Lashkar organization travelled with Masood's convoy of vehicles. It took them several weeks to reach Kandahar from the border of Pakistan. It was at this time that Jagan had an opportunity to observe from close quarters Ahmed Shah Masood's imposing presence, sharpness of intellect and progressive views.

Already, Maulana had pointed out the regressive thinking of many of the groups in relation to women. Later, during their training under the Lashkars, Amir was dissatisfied with their focussing only on Kashmir, and not having a global view of things.

At the same time, they did not fail to attract Ahmed Shah's attention. Noticing in particular, Jagan's fluency in English, he enquired about him in detail.

It was at this time, that the Soviet Union acknowledged its defeat. Within the Union itself, there were strident voices heard against the war. Hence, many were of the view that very soon the Soviet troops would retreat from Afghanistan. Under such circumstances, more than the strength of the arms, political power, and statesmanship determined the status of each rebel group. It was a time when American intervention too was increasing in Afghanistan.

There was a need at such times, for people who had a good knowledge of English and communication skills. That was why Ahmed Shah Masood enquired about Jagan and his antecedents with interest. During those few days, he did not behave like a big leader, and all of them interacted as comrades and peers. Thus, Jagan became quite intimate with Ahmed Shah. He engaged in several philosophical arguments with him. Jagan appreciated his foresightedness and progressive bent of mind.

When they reached Kandahar, the two of them expressed their desire to be with Ahmed Shah Masood. He too, took them happily under his large wings. Not only that; he often took Jagan with him to various meetings.

All roads lead to Rome, they say; similarly, all rivers flow towards the sea. Likewise, it was a time when all Mujahideen organizations converged on Kabul. These moves were based on the premise, that when the Soviet Union left Afghanistan, whoever was in control of Kabul would form the government. Men like Hekmatyar functioned only with their own interests in mind. Because of this competition for seizing power, the internal differences in the organizations, differences in their doctrines, the leaders' dominance, their egos, and greed for power began to surface. In the meanwhile, countries like America, Saudi Arabia, Pakistan, and Iran engaged in a shadow war through various groups, for retaining their regional interest in independent Afghanistan.

Ahmed Shah Masood differed slightly from this. He was firm in his stand that only after an interim government, made up of the representatives of all the organizations was established, could anyone assume control over Kabul. Hence, although his troops were stationed close to Kabul, he avoided an attack on the city. Hekmatyar, who probably mistook his patience for weakness, conducted rocket attacks on Kabul, and subjected the ordinary civilians to great misery.

It was under these circumstances that hectic talks were held in Peshawar. During these talks, hard bargains were struck with the support of the

United Nations. In this situation, Hekmatyar consented to the solution proposed, on one hand to bide his time, and on the other, he augmented his military strength and tried to move towards Kabul, exploiting things to his advantage.

Simultaneous with the direct attacks that he launched, Hekmatyar had also sent many small groups to murder Ahmed Shah Masood. Most of them were identified before they approached Masood and were liquidated. One of them succeeded in reaching him.

Jagan could never forget that day. The enemies, who had intruded into their camps, had begun their attacks at midnight. Suddenly, the sounds of the bombs exploding and guns being fired could be heard.

Waking up instantly, Jagan gathered his arms, and collecting Ahmed Shah, who was in the adjacent tent, ran fast into the neighbouring bushes.

After a few hours of gunfire, Shah's men succeeded in driving away the intruders, and regained control of the camp. In the light of the dawn, they were able to assess the total damage caused by the attack. Two of the intruders lay dead, close to Shah's tent. Only then, Masood realized that he had escaped due to Jagan's timely action. Accustomed, as he was to face external attacks until then, it was a new experience for Masood to counter an attack from within. Though they had been given intensive training to crush external attacks, and they had drawn up contingency plans to be executed in a disciplined manner, they did not expect attacks to come from within. Normally, Mujahideen groups are the aggressors, and not at the receiving end of attacks from intruders.

Until noon that day, they conducted mopping up operations looking for intruders and destroying them. In the course of their search, they found Amir's body. They were not able to determine whether Amir was one of the intruders or one who faced them.

Whatever be the case, Jagan felt as if the whole world was in darkness, having lost his only friend.

After this incident, Masood became very friendly with him. Wherever he went, he took Jagan with him. The latter was more like his personal security guard.

The Mujahideen organizations, which had focused on their collective success until they gained it, now, began to jostle for the authority and power which that victory would bestow on them. Under these circumstances, everyone was confused as to who was a friend and who an enemy.

Another incident could be mentioned, as evidence of Masood's negotiating skill. Rasheed Dostum, an Uzbekistani General, was won over and began helping Ahmed Shah.

As days went by, Ahmed Shah's popularity spread all over the land. Hence, he was given importance in the interim government. He was made the Defence Minister. Hekmatyar was not amenable to reason, and was bent on taking the path of destruction. Nevertheless, Ahmed Shah's prowess and foresight prevented Hekmatyar from having an upper hand.

At this time, Jagan was at the portals of Kabul. Like a plant that had been uprooted and transplanted in another soil, he engrossed himself completely in the current affairs of Afghanistan.

Having identified himself as an Afghan, Jagan concentrated on carrying out his daily duties. Hence, he felt as if his old relationships and memories had deserted him.

He felt as though incidents such as his coming to India and his being imprisoned, had taken place in his previous birth. Hence, of late, he had no desire to return to Australia.

The faces of Maulana and Amir appeared occasionally in his dreams. He thought he had fulfilled Maulana's wish that he should join Ahmed Shah Masood.

Jagan realized that he had encountered innumerable dangers within a short period. He had witnessed many deaths with his own eyes. However, until then, he had never killed anyone even accidentally.

I am the Lord

With a weapon in his hand, Jagan reflected. What is the meaning of life? A man, who is alive today, is dead tomorrow. Human life being so uncertain, why do men harbour rivalry and jealousy between themselves? When he thought, that if he knew the answer to this question, he could himself establish a new religion, a smile blossomed on his face!

Ezhuth Aani

# PART II

# PATH

I am the Lord

# 1

"The Lord will save you; the Lord will save you." Hearing this voice, Jagan looked around to see where it came from.A tall, majestic man in a white dress stood there. His demeanour and magnetism attracted him.

A pacific and serene face, a smile hovered on his lips. In a pure white dress, he appeared strangely radiant. So far, in prison, all the foreigners who met him had indulged only in questioning, drilling, and torturing him. He wondered how this man alone could be so very loving. He expressed his thought instantly.

"I am an Islamic militant. Why do you not hate me?"

"God so loved the world that He gave His only begotten Son, that whoever believes in Him shall not perish, but have eternal life. When you know me better, you will understand this in course of time. You are going to receive a wonderful gift freely."

So saying, he thrust a copy of the Bible into his hands. He asked him to read the chapter John 14 of the book.

"I shall return in two days. If you have any doubt we shall talk about them."

Ezhuth Aani

"This is God's Word. Every word in this has been uttered by God, or inspired by Him. It has been handed down for 1600 years, written by almost forty people. But, though there may be differences in the tone, language, and practice, it is a continuous story. It's because of this, that I say that God has written this book. Every word in this is the Truth. If you read this, the problems in your life will disappear, and you'll attain everlasting bliss.

"This is the only book in the world that has been written by God. Though many men have written it over several centuries, there are no contradictions in this. Thirty eight times in this book, it has been recorded that God spoke this. No other book has this evidence.

"Many of the events mentioned in this book have been proved historically. Some of the major incidents recorded in this book have been proved through the clues obtained from archaeological research conducted during the past 200 years.

"Incidents which had been predicted in this book have been proved later. The coming of Jesus has been mentioned several centuries earlier, at the beginning of the Bible. The sacrifice of Jesus has been pointed out quite early, through the story of Isaac. If you read this very sacred book with sincere devotion, all your wishes, longings, and desires will be fulfilled.

I am the Lord

"You read this book, my son. I shall teach you the ways of elevating yourself in life."

So saying, he blessed Jagan and took leave. From that day, there was a change in the way he was treated. He was still one among the prisoners. But they had stopped torturing him completely. Similarly, there was an improvement in the quality and quantity of the food served. He was given more freedom to exercise and read newspapers.

The stranger visited Jagan once every few days. Nowadays, he brought him different kinds of gifts. He was given food items, a radio, clothes, and so on; slowly, his life began to change for the better.

Jagan too, found the Gospel interesting. Beginning with John, he read the gospels of Matthew, Mark, and Luke quite fast. Ever since he came to this prison, the only person who spoke to him frankly and sympathetically was that man. Hence, every day Jagan awaited his arrival eagerly.

After some time, he gave Jagan some homework. He must imbibe all that he read and answer the questions given. Then, the man would come and discuss them.

For one who had been subjected to assault and torture every day, this was very heaven. Instead of every moment passing like an era, now time passed quickly.

Ezhuth Aani

As he read more and more about Jesus in the New Testament, Jagan felt a unique upsurge of emotions. What a man! No, no, He was God. Only God can forgive those who killed Him. It is not possible for an ordinary man. Thus, various thoughts ran through his mind. Who can hate Jesus? Was He not a sublime Being?

Some time was spent in learning about Jesus Christ. Only once, he asked him a question. Both Matthew and Luke had mentioned Christ's lineage. In this, after David, the two lists were very different. Jagan asked him about this.

Only then, he came to know about his other side. "Had you read the book with devotion, such questions would not have arisen in your mind. There is a flaw in your piety." So saying, he paced up and down the room. His face was red. His forehead had beads of perspiration on it. His attitude was severe.

After remaining silent for a while, he said, "Among the two, one is Joseph's lineage, and the other is Mary's. If you had read the book sincerely, such questions will not arise in your mind." When he looked at Jagan sharply, the latter cast his eyes down, fearing to face him directly then, with a victorious smile, the man said, "My son, one who follows Christ needs to be humble. Meekness and humility is necessary. Do not challenge God's word by asking questions. If you have a doubt, you are at fault. The Bible is the Truth. Hereafter, don't ask foolish questions like this."

I am the Lord

He then began to speak to Jagan lovingly, as before.

After that incident, Jagan stopped asking questions. He began to think that there was a lapse in his devotion, whenever he had a doubt.

The account in Matthew, of King Herod's killing of all the children in the land fearing a prophecy, the Immaculate Conception, and Christ's birth in a stable, were all reminiscent of Lord Krishna's birth. But Jagan did not dare to ask any question about that.

If there was no such thing as a question, there would have been no progress at all in this world. Whenever man stops asking questions, he surrenders absolutely. This was Jagan's condition now.

Thus, every day, his perceptions kept changing systematically. Pastor Robert also encouraged him to read the rest of the New Testament. Having read the four gospels, Jagan was astonished at what a noble person Christ was. This astonishment produced in him an expectation of happiness and peace.

Suddenly, one day Pastor Robert asked Jagan to read a book called Daniel. This was the first book in the Old Testament that he was going to read.

Daniel, the story of a Jewish prophet, was very powerful. The King of Babylon, Nebuchadnezzar, subjugated Israel and Judah, and was considered as a great king in the world. He ridiculed the God of Israel, and compelled everyone to worship himself. Apart from this, he had a huge golden statue installed in the middle of the city, and ordered that every time his servants sounded a herald, people must leave all their work, fall at the feet of the statue and worship it. Whoever disobeyed this order was burnt alive.

Three Jewish youth refused to worship this idol, and hence, were thrown into a furnace. Instead of being burnt, they danced in joy. Hence, the king accepted the superiority of the Jewish God.

The book of Daniel also has a story of the King's dream. The king had a strange dream one night. A huge statue, with its head made of gold, chest of silver, abdomen of bronze, and legs made of iron and clay, appeared in his dream. A stone that came from somewhere, hit the statue, which broke into pieces. None was able to explain the significance of this dream. Only Daniel could.

All the empires in this world will be destroyed one day. Subsequently, Christ's eternal empire will be established. This is the meaning of the dream, said Daniel.

I am the Lord

At this point, Pastor Robert asked, "Which, do you think, are the empires made of gold, silver, bronze, iron, and clay?"

Jagan waited eagerly for his answer. The Pastor said, "The part made of gold is Babylonia. The silver chest is the Persian Empire. The one that succeeded it is the Greek empire. The last one is the Roman empire."

"It is several centuries since the Roman empire fell, is it not?"

"The present states of America, England, Germany, and other Western countries are all a continuation of the Roman empire. Just as there are ten toes on our feet, they continue to exist in different forms."

"But," said Robert, peering at Jagan.

Unable to bear the sharpness of his look, the youngster cast his eyes on the ground.

"The day when the Lord's Kingdom shall come to earth, is not far off. This is the good Word that I shall give you. We shall stop with this today. Until next week, keep recollecting what I've said. And read some more pages of this."

Those pages contained a dream about a tree, and its explanation. In the dream, there is a huge tree with branches reaching the sky. Its leaves are beautiful. Its widespread branches were home to several birds. Suddenly, a messenger descended from the sky, and said; 'Cut off the branches of this tree. Bind its trunk alone with iron and bronze, and leave it open to the elements, to wear out in the heat and cold. Let it be in the garden for seven years, as one with the animals and birds'.

The explanation of that dream was also given in it. According to it, the king wanders for seven years, not being in his proper senses. Later, he pleads with God, gets His pardon, and regains his old life.

As this calculation of seven years appeared to match Jagan's state, he felt as if he were electrified. His going to India, then his becoming a Muslim, and now a helpless prisoner – everything seemed to agree well with the story of the fallen tree. It was nearly six years since his wanderings began. He could not but compare his condition with that of the tree.

He waited eagerly for the day of Pastor Robert's next visit. Nowadays, he had lost interest in offering prayers five times a day.

Though he paid lip service to Allah, his thoughts were only about what Pastor Robert had said and what he would say. He felt a kind of enthusiasm that his six years' ordeal would soon end.

Waiting for something to happen, Jagan's mind was always in an excited state. He could feel that a change was taking place in his life. He also realized that he had absolutely no strength to arrest that change. He felt that a superhuman force was directing his life. Novelty everywhere, eagerness in everything – every new day brought in a new confidence. Nowadays, he could not bring himself to deal with the guards roughly, as before. He had an illusion that everywhere there was serenity and peace.

The guards too understood the changes in Jagan. Changes could be noticed in their behaviour also. They began to treat him cordially. As per the philosophy, 'Do unto others what you would have others do unto you', an understanding began to develop between Jagan and the security guards. He realized that they were merely doing their duty, and did not have any personal rancour against him.

The next time the Pastor came, he discussed things with him lovingly. Now, he did not sit with him and read the Bible. He gave him a task. That is, to read the seventh chapter of Daniel and then read John's prophecy in Revelation. He asked Jagan to analyse both, find out if there was any connection between the two, and then put down his observations. He gave him seven days' time.

In the seventh chapter, Daniel has a dream. In it, four animals, namely, a lion, a bear, a leopard, and a dragon come one after the other, and play havoc with the world. Finally, the Lord defeated them, and established an eternal kingdom.

Ezhuth Aani

Subsequently, one like the Son of Man appears among the clouds. The Lord bestows on him the right to rule this world forever. People belonging to all the countries, and those speaking all the languages kneel and worship him.

The last animal, the dragon, is very powerful. It will dominate the entire world and keep it under its control. The war waged to destroy it, will be terrible.

Having completed this, Jagan began reading the chapter 'Revelation'. Until now, Pastor Robert's methods of teaching were like listening to a story and reading it. Now, for the first time, he had to read for himself, understand it and then explain what he learnt to the Pastor. He accepted this as a big responsibility. That is, for the first time, he had been given the freedom to think independently. It gave him great joy. He did not realize that he had been given only limited freedom; i.e., to move within a circle. He did not understand that Pastor Robert was trying to extract from Jagan's mouth, the words which he wanted him to utter.

In the book, Revelation, seven visions have been described. They appeared to John in the form of dreams. Jesus Christ appears on a white horse, with seven stars and a shining sword. After this, John is presented before the Lord's throne. There are 24 chosen saints standing. Four animals (lion, bull, man and eagle) are singing praises of God.

I am the Lord

Subsequently, seven sealed manuscripts are seen on the right side of God. Only the holy Lamb has the authority to break the seal and read the manuscripts. With the breaking of each seal, progressive waves of destruction would engulf the world. It describes the seven-headed dragon, the beast from the sea and from the earth.

The bearers of the beast's number (666) would be doomed. At this point, the Lamb appears with 144000 faithful. The Son of God appears with a sword and harvests God's wrath. Blood flows like a river. The seven bowls of wrath would be fulfilled. Babylon would fall. After the Last War, the Lord's Empire will be established.

A thousand years later, Satan will wage a second war. After his final defeat, God's eternal kingdom will be established on earth. Dead will be resurrected and presented before the Lord for Justice. The good will be eternally happy. They will not experience any sorrow or need.

Those who do not repent and seek forgiveness will suffer eternal hell and burning fires.

This is the summary of the chapter 'Revelation' as understood by Jagan. What is the connection between this and what Daniel wrote? It is that the kingdoms raised by Man are impermanent. The Revelation of John is more or less the same as those prophesied by Daniel 600 years earlier. But John's account is more detailed, and instils fear by bringing in the concept of an eternal Hell.

Ezhuth Aani

The next time he met Pastor Robert, Jagan expressed his awe and his opinion. Also, he asked him what the true import of those prophecies was.

The Pastor said, "Don't worry, my son. You will not understand this directly. Gradually you will understand it. I will explain it to you. Some of these prophecies have already come true. We are approaching the final stage. Before that, try to redeem yourself from your sins. Otherwise, you'll meet your end, and fall into burning fire and suffer eternally."

"What should I do then? I have not committed any sin knowingly. How will I go to Hell?"

"Here is where you err. All of us are sinners. Christ has said, 'I am the way and the truth and the life. No one comes to the Father except through me.' Hence, without accepting Jesus, you cannot go to Heaven."

"Muslims also accept Christ as a messenger of God. Why then do you say that I don't accept Him?" asked Jagan.

"My son read the book Romans. Then you'll understand."

I am the Lord

# 2

The book called Epistles written to the Romans is a very important one. In this, the Paul gives an explanation regarding Christ's crucifixion. Paul belonged to the ruling Jewish elite. Bearing the name of Saul, he used to hunt down Christ's followers, and inflict all kinds of sufferings on them. Finally, on his way to Damascus, he loses his eyesight. Then Jesus appears to him and restores his eyesight. He recognizes him as an apostle.

Subsequently, Paul goes to different parts of the known world, and reorganizes Christian worship into a religion with a proper framework. The most important tenets of the Christian Church are as follows:

1. Man has been created by God as an image of Himself.

2. By committing the first sin of tasting the forbidden apple, Adam loses his eternity, and is condemned to a life that must end in death.

3. Because of Adam's sin, the whole of mankind is tainted. Now, all of us are born as sinners.

4. Later, the Lord sends His only Son, Jesus Christ, in human form.

5. Jesus Christ, the Son of God, was tortured and killed.

6. Jesus Christ, who was crucified, rose to life again on the third day.

7. Christ's life was the price paid to wash away the sins of mankind.

8. The only way to redeem ourselves from our sins is to accept Jesus and surrender unto Him.

9. In the end, we will all be presented to God. Then, only those who accepted Him and led good lives will be chosen for eternal bliss.

10. The rest will have to suffer burning fires, everlastingly.

This philosophy was propounded by St. Paul. Due to his untiring work, the Christian movement spread across many countries, and later emerged as a major religion. It was because of Paul that continuity was established between the Old and the New Testaments. After several centuries, Emperor Constantine embraced Christianity and the Old and the New Testaments were combined, and the

I am the Lord

Bible as a complete book was canonised. In the New Testament, apart from the Gospels of Matthew, Mark, Luke, and John, most of the other portions are letters written by St. Paul to the pioneers of the Christian Church in various countries.

Much later, the American president Thomas Jefferson, and British scholars like George Bernard Shaw and Priestley criticized Paul very strongly. Their accusation was that Paul had modified Christ's teachings, and imposed his own thoughts and opinions.

Be that as it may, the Epistles written by Paul to the Romans constitute a separate book. This forms the basis of the Christian doctrine.

As Jagan read the book 'Romans', he felt a great change in himself.

Dying in Jesus and being born again in his own form, was a new concept for Jagan. That is, that he could discard the old, and as in a new birth, live a blissful life leaving behind all sorrows, produced in him a great desire. It was a new message that he could be re-born, and lead a noble life. A good message for him. However, he could not understand two things. First, why does Paul say that all men are sinners? Second, how could Christ's crucifixion and sacrifice redeem us from our sins? Though these two questions arose in his mind, he was scared to ask Pastor Robert about this.

Ezhuth Aani

It was then, that the Pastor obtained permission from the authorities and took him out. Only then, he realized that he was in Spain. Initially, only once a week he took him out in his Mercedes Benz. The first time he left the prison and went out with him, it was a delightful experience for Jagan.

The first time he went out, he felt the free air after several months, and along with that joy, he was amazed at the Spanish architecture and the stunning natural scenes. Paella, a local dish was a relief to him. Having been used to only bread and meat in the prison, this was like ambrosia to him. Moreover, the manner in which the restaurant workers respected Pastor Robert produced in him a great regard for the elder. This was despite the fact that the first two times, the Pastor never spoke to him about religious matters. He asked Jagan personal questions very affectionately. He asked him about the incidents, which took place in India after his arrest, rather casually than with the intention of extracting information from him out of curiosity. Because of this, Jagan's confidence in him and love for him increased further.

At the same time, he continued to read the Bible. As requested by the Pastor, he began to read the part 'Genesis'. Gradually, he lost interest in Islamic worship. He also wore a Cross given by the Pastor on a chain around his neck.

Jagan was greatly moved by the huge Gothic cathedral called La Sagrada Familia, created by the renowned Spanish architect Antony Gaudi. Like Viswakarma, Gaudi was also considered as God's architect. The buildings, which were the products of his unique imaginative power, and which enhanced the beauty of Barcelona, could be seen here and there, standing majestically. Gaudi incorporated into his buildings not only natural scenes, but also geometrical shapes such as ellipses, very aesthetically. His creations like Casa Mila and Casa Batllo amazed Jagan by the intricacy of the designs skilfully woven into every part of the structure. Gaudi's crowning glory, the church called La Sagrada Familia, inspired and excited Jagan the most. This building had not yet been completed. Unfortunately, during its construction Gaudi died in an accident, unexpectedly. Later, even the last copy of the blueprint personally prepared by Gaudi, was destroyed by General Franco's henchmen. Subsequently, due to various reasons including the Civil War in Spain, the construction of the church was delayed. Nevertheless, it overcame all the obstacles and now stands tall and majestic. It may take some more years for completion, but by this creation, Gaudi had earned an everlasting place in the history of architecture.

Giving details of Gaudi, Pastor Robert avoided talking about religion. However, he mentioned Gaudi's devotion to God very respectfully. He made it clear implicitly to Jagan, that only if a man has devotion to God, he can achieve remarkable things.

Every time the Pastor went out with Jagan, he took him to an eatery. Dishes prepared with tomatoes, eggplants, garlic, mushrooms, and whole gram, cooked in olive oil and spiced with hot pepper, were very tasty and different. Bread and pasta were the important food items of the Catalonians.

Gradually, Jagan avoided eating food only after questioning if it was prepared the 'halaal' way. Similarly, he reduced offering Islamic worship, and was more interested in reading the Bible.

Pastor Robert and Jagan visited various places and became very friendly with each other. Once, they went to Museu Picasso, the museum containing Pablo Picasso's paintings.

Picasso lived in Barcelona from 1895 for nine years. Even after that, he visited the city occasionally, and maintained his connections there. This museum containing Picasso's works had been housed in five palaces, built during the 13th and 14th centuries. Thousands of Picasso's creations were in this museum. They included paintings, which Picasso had drawn under different mental conditions. In particular, the ones that were created during the tragic phase in his life, called the 'blue period', appeared to reflect Jagan's mood, and hence, attracted him greatly. Apart from this, the 58 paintings in the collection called Las Meninas were also displayed in this museum.

I am the Lord

For a few years after his friend's suicide, the paintings that Picasso created in a dejected mood, were mostly in colours like blue, and were reflective of his mental state.

Later one day, they went to a cathedral in Barcelona. That 700 year-old building overawed Jagan. Then, Pastor Robert asked Jagan, "Do you know that at one time the whole Iberian Peninsula was controlled by Muslims? After the Western Roman Empire declined in the 5th century, a tribe called Visigoths ruled this area. Then, from the 8th century onwards, for several centuries it was under Muslim dominance. The present Spain and Portugal are in the Iberian Peninsula. But fortunately, the northern hilly regions including Barcelona did not come under their rule." So saying, he looked at Jagan closely.

"My son, Christianity and Islam have been at war ever since. But, ultimately Jesus Christ will win." As Jagan kept looking at the ground silently, Pastor Robert said, "This is not your fault. You are a scapegoat. You have been dragged into this war by circumstances. But ..." he stopped.

"But," Jagan looked at him eagerly.

"No incident happens without reason in life. God has a plan for every one of us. In His great play, all of us have our own small roles. Depending on our integrity and hard work, we will be given our responsibilities in God's eternal Kingdom."

Ezhuth Aani

Jagan interrupted him saying, "I'm not a Christian!"

"God has come searching for you. It is up to you to accept or reject Him," said the Pastor.

"As far as I know, whichever religion one belongs to, doing Good is equal to worshipping God, is it not?" asked Jagan.

"Not at all. Only by accepting Jesus Christ in your life, can you obtain redemption. Did you not read the 14$^{th}$ chapter of John and the 'Romans'?" asked the Pastor.

"Only if I commit any sin, will I become a sinner. I have not committed any sin knowingly, so far."

The Pastor's eyes reddened. "There is no place in Heaven for one who is not humble and faithful. Let this be the last occasion of your asking me questions. Had you read 'Romans' devoutly, you would have understood. God created Adam the first Man, in His own image. Because of his sin, all his descendants have been cursed. All of us are sinners at birth. There is no exception to this. Having cursed mankind, God in His infinite mercy, sent His only Son as a pure man. Only by washing our sins with the sacrifices of this Son of God, can we get redemption and protection. Only if you let Christ into your life and place Him in your heart will you get eternity; otherwise, you'll die and suffer in Hell."

I am the Lord

Saying this, he remained silent for some time. Then looking at Jagan, he said, "Before you ask the question I'll give you one more answer. It is customary for Satan to sow a question like this in the minds of Doubting Thomases like you. That is, that there is no mention of Christ in the Old Testament. This is wrong. Read the story of Isaac in the Genesis. It tells how Abraham takes his son Isaac, to be sacrificed. Isaac himself carried the wood for his funeral. But, at the last minute, instead of Isaac God sacrifices a lamb. It was caught in the thorny bushes. What do you learn from this?"

Before he could answer, Pastor Robert said, "We are all in the same condition as Isaac. But God sacrifices His own Son in place of the lamb. Christ wearing a crown of thorns and carrying the wooden Cross has been predicted. There are numerous examples like this, to show that God promised the redemption at that time itself, for sending His Son for our sake."

He continued: "Tomorrow I leave for America. I shall return in a month. You read the Bible. I have not taken you around so far, expecting something in return. But I have the work of saving some other souls. Before I return, make up your mind. Jesus calls you. If you are not ready this time, never mind. We can see later.

"God loves you. His love is eternal. He is patient. Only when you are ready to embrace Him, will He accept you. You must understand one thing. Only when you accept Jesus, all your desires will be fulfilled. Until then, however good you are, you will not get what you want. The Lord's protection is being offered to you freely. But you should prepare yourself to receive it.

"If you accept Christ, I shall recommend your release myself. Moreover, you will get the opportunity to help me in the service of God."

I am the Lord

# 3

After Pastor Robert left, Jagan felt for the first time, the pangs of separation. Even when he left his parents to go to India, he had never had such a feeling. He was completely overwhelmed by Pastor Robert's smile and the confidence that he infused in him. Days passed into weeks, and one month was over. When the Pastor was not there, he was not given any special concessions. It was 'back to square one' — the same solitude, the same food. He understood clearly, that only if he obeyed what the Pastor had said, he would win his freedom. As there was nothing else to do, he read the Holy Bible repeatedly. Gradually, he lost his hold and interest in Islamic tradition. He stopped Islamic worship altogether.

He decided that he would change his religion.

When he realized how he had been enslaved by Pastor Robert's dominance, he felt on one hand an unknown sense of calm, and on the other, a sense of fear and trepidation. The peace that comes, when one does not feel any responsibility in anything, and entrusts oneself completely to God saying, 'Thy Will be done', now took hold of Jagan. When he thought of how, due to the unexpected occurrences that took place in his life, here he was in an oppressive state, in a strange country, and treading a new path, he felt intimidated and apprehensive. At the same time, when he thought that Robert was a messenger sent by God for his liberation, gratitude and confidence filled his mind.

It was some time, since the courage and self-confidence with which he had steered his life within the limits he had set for himself, had deserted him. When he decided that henceforth he would let things happen as Robert willed, and that he would remain 'passive', an extraordinary peace of mind took hold of him.

When man gives up striving (to achieve something), and leaves everything to a higher Power, it is natural for his mind to feel light. An effort involves feelings such as fear, anger, anxiety, and uncertainty. If one steps aside from acting autonomously, and allows life to go on in its own path, there will be neither excessive suffering nor desire. Jagan experienced this now. He felt the illusion that the changes, which came over him, were due to the new path proposed by Pastor Robert. It seemed to him that these feelings were produced in reality, because of his reading the Bible.

Whatever the case may be, once a decision is taken, it is difficult to think of other options. Similarly, Jagan's mind was now full of the thoughts of when Pastor Robert would come, and what he (Jagan) would say to him. Like a wife awaiting the arrival of her husband, or a son that of

I am the Lord

his father, Jagan waited eagerly for the arrival of Pastor Robert.

Somehow, that one month passed very, very slowly. As promised, after a month, the guard announced that he had a guest and took him. Who else would come to visit him? Deep down in his mind, he had a longing – why did he not have any other relationships.

Instead of taking him to the usual visitors' room, the guard took him to a different building. Unlike a usual prison complex, it was a beautiful place of worship. There, Jagan saw the prison warden, James, whom he had seen earlier only on the day he had been brought to this prison. Now he was seeing him again. Apart from him, there were guards, workers, and prisoners too, like Jagan. They could be identified as prisoners, only by their blue uniform. Some of them had dense beards. Some were clean-shaven. Jagan touched his beard. Only then, he realized that one by one he was losing his Islamic identification marks and traditions. This beard was the lone sign of his old life. Must definitely remove it tomorrow morning, he decided.

When he entered, Pastor Robert was talking to some of the others. He appeared not to take notice of Jagan's entry at all. The youth was not only disappointed, but also jealous of those with whom the Pastor was talking. He was himself astonished at the change that had come over him. There was a time when he had no worry on earth, and did not care for anybody. Now, here he was, craving for someone's attention. He could not control the surge of thoughts that rose in his mind.

Just then, Pastor Robert got on to the stage. 'Silence! Silence!' he said. As if by some magic, there was pin-drop silence.

"Friends, you have all been chosen by God to do His service. You have all been born in different countries, lived different lives, involved by Satan in misdeeds at various stages of your lives; and then repenting, and being reformed, been brought here. I shall pray to the Almighty Lord that hereafter your life should be prosperous."

For two hours, there were sermons, songs, prayers and so on. Then, lunch was served. Nobody questioned whether the food had been prepared the 'halaal' way. As though they had been starving for days, they feasted, serving themselves different varieties of dishes in their plates. Thanks were offered, before and after lunch. Jagan too ate different types of food.

They were made to eat at different tables, with ten to twelve men at each table.

Pastor Robert went to each table, and conversed freely with many of them. Finally, when he came to Jagan's table, the latter stood up. As if he saw him only then, the Pastor asked him, "How are you, my friend?"

I am the Lord

As though he had been waiting for this moment, and with tears in his eyes, he said, "I have been waiting for you. But you did not even notice me."

"My son, I have several things to do. I must save many more souls like you. But, God has not forgotten you."

"I've decided to convert. When can I be baptized?" asked Jagan.

The Pastor looked at him closely. "You cannot be converted so easily. First, you must prove that you are worthy of God. Jesus will convert you systematically. Do not be in a hurry, my friend! When the time comes, we'll know about it. After you have become a mature man, you shall be converted."

So saying, he appointed an Englishman, Paul, one of the twelve at Jagan's table, as the group leader.

He told them, "The twelve of you shall gather together every day, engage in such activities as reading the Bible, praying, doing social service, taking the Good News to others and so on. You shall help to establish God's Kingdom on earth. May God bless you. After you have cleansed yourself of your sins, you will receive God's pardon and protection."

Ezhuth Aani

Then, Paul spoke. "I was also a sinner like you. Pastor Robert saved me. That experience is ennobling. You can know it only through experience. The Holy Spirit will be with you and lead you."

They then dispersed. That whole night Jagan could not sleep. On one hand, in a corner of his brain, an unknown fear entered slowly. 'Will every Movement be like this? Forsaking family life, meditating all the twenty four hours on what the leader said, reading the Movement's philosophy again and again, engaging in (controlled) debates only with a select few, doing social service, using the good reputation earned from it to carry the Leader's message to more people, and taking those attracted by this to the Leader — such work is also done by political organizations like the Naxalites. Christian, Muslim, and Hindu propagandists also do the same. The philosophies may be different; the policies may be different. The procedures are the same. Who are the beneficiaries of all this, nobody knows. However, for those engaged in this wholly, it becomes their vocation and lifestyle'.

On the other hand, although he was doubtful about whether he was being brainwashed, he also knew only too well, that he had no other alternative.

He remembered Pastor Robert telling him, 'Doubts are an indication of your faith's immaturity'. He reprimanded himself, thinking

I am the Lord

that such doubts arose only because he was a sinner.

He spent the whole night in being half-asleep, tossing and turning, and then sitting up thinking. Somehow, the rays of the sun that entered his room through the window dispelled the darkness and woke him up.

The first thing that he did on getting up in the morning was to shave his beard. The security men who noticed this when he went for his breakfast, were very friendly towards him. They were quite happy that he had altered his appearance to become one with them.

Subsequently, changes began to occur in his life. He was allotted a room in another building. He was allowed to roam freely in that building now. But if he wanted to go out, it was only with Paul and the other group members.

Every day of the week, they were given some duty. According to a timetable, on Mondays they had to clean and decorate the church; on Tuesdays they had to meet the other prisoners and explain the Gospel to them; giving them the Bible written in Arabic and Urdu. At such times, it was common for the prisoners to spit on them and refuse to accept the book. On Wednesdays, it was confession and obtaining pardon. On Thursdays, it was reading the Bible and engaging in limited discussions. Most of these were like reading the Bible through Robert's eyes only. That is, Paul taught them verses from the Bible exactly as Pastor Robert had done.

Every Sunday, Pastor Robert taught Paul and the other group leaders what they should read during the coming week, and what they should discuss and how. On Fridays and Saturdays, the groups went to the hospitals in Barcelona, and to the bus and train terminals, and engaged themselves in religious propaganda and in selling books.

Jagan was astonished to see big glossy beautiful books being sold very cheap. How was this possible? Does this organization get funds in other ways? He gave up that thought on the ground, that he was not qualified to analyse the economics of religious organizations.

On Sundays, all the groups, which belonged to that church, gathered together and offered prayers, led by Pastor Robert. He would sermonize on selected parts of each chapter of the Bible, explaining them with illustrations. In between, there would be singing of hymns. This worship would go on for hours. Then lunch would be served amidst discussions, and the whole day would be spent thus.

Jagan had given up his Islamic ways completely. Although he was sad at some sort of parting, he also felt a kind of freedom from rigid rules and regulations. Not altogether though.

I am the Lord

Occasionally, he felt that he had merely been dragged from one sort of control into another.

His new life gave him a kind of awe as well as an expectation. But the Confession and Forgiveness that took place on Wednesdays produced a kind of fear in him. On those days, along with his twelve group members there would be some others also. They would wear clothes with Mandarin collars similar to what pastors wear. Some of them would have video and audio equipment with them. Initially, Pastor Robert appeared in person, sometimes.

"Friends, Truth shall set you free. God knows all your thoughts and deeds. Whether you had illegal sex with a woman, or merely looked at her lustfully, both are sins. All of us are sinners. Only if we acknowledge our sins openly, and ask for pardon repenting our wrongs, will we be saved. All of us belong to the same family. As we die in Jesus and are re-born, we have become brothers in the eyes of the Lord. There should be no secrets amongst us. By sharing our sins every day, we offer the burden of our disgrace and feelings of guilt to God, and acquire a sense of liberation," said Robert.

After this, one by one their confessions began. Those who did not belong to their group did not talk about their sins. Pastor Robert introduced them only as his assistants.

Ezhuth Aani

Initially, though it was uneasy to share one's personal matters with others openly, when one or two began to speak about themselves, it appeared to be a common practice. Overcoming their hesitation, the members started sharing their misdeeds quite eagerly. When one is stripped in public, one would feel disgraced at first. If everyone were to be nude, there would be no place for any shame. It was the same with them. Gradually they lost their inhibitions.

Pastor Robert said, "We present ourselves before God, clad only in the garb of righteousness laid down by Him. Was He not the One who gave us, who were nude, a dress to wear?"

Motivated by such words, the desire to lay bare all their thoughts and deeds without any inhibitions, took hold of all of them.

If a man wishes to retain his identity, he should not transgress certain personal limits. But here, the members were losing their identity in that of the group. However, in their current mental condition, this appeared to be the right path to them.

I am the Lord

# 4

Today was his turn. That he was going to disclose all his personal matters frightened him greatly, but at the same time excited him also.

In the first few weeks, he had heard the others' confessions, and hence, he had become accustomed to the process. They shared their thoughts and deeds, which had been lying dormant deep down in their minds, with the others. Initially, it sounded a bit disgusting. Soon the disgust gave way to an attractive, pleasurable, addictive feeling. He noticed that once they shared their innermost thoughts with the others, they felt relieved of their burden, and experienced a sense of freedom and liberation.

Repeatedly, Pastor Robert and Paul told the group very firmly, 'We are all one family. There are no secrets between us; there shouldn't be also'. Gradually, it became a routine for him to listen to others' personal intimacies and share his own with them, unabashedly.

He described how he had been rescued by the disciples of an Islamic religious leader; how he embraced Islam; how he escaped along with them; how he went to Dharmabad crossing forests, mountain ranges and rivers; how he escaped from the train riots and reached Gujarat through secret routes; later, how with his friends he commandeered the drug traffickers' ship; how when they tried to cross the Indian naval borders, the Indian navy shot their ship; how they struggled in the sea; how Maulana whom he respected greatly, died in his arms; how Amir and he vowed to be friends as per Maulana's dying wish, and finally, how they reached Afghanistan via Lahore.

When he began narrating about his links with the Islamic militants, some of the men who introduced themselves as Pastor Robert's assistants started questioning him. Although everything was done under the cloak of a confession, their curiosity surprised him. Just as it is immaterial for a man who is already wet, whether he gets wetter or wettest, and 'come what may' was Jagan's attitude. He had neither the interest nor the energy to ask why they were curious. In particular, they grilled him on details as to who he was in communication with; the places where he had been put up; where he crossed the Pakistan border and entered Afghanistan; who were the people he met there; what was the connection between him and Ahmed Shah Masood; what was the connection between Masood and the others, and so on.

******

In April 1992, a 'never-before' opportunity was presented to Afghanistan, but the tragedy of its having been squandered was also staged.

I am the Lord

As Jagan was fluent in spoken English, he was used for communicating with Western diplomats, journalists, and arms dealers. They were not confident enough to leave him alone. Hence, there were always two bodyguards with him. Though they were supposed to give him protection, he knew very well that they were his guardsmen. Thinking that gradually they would come to trust him, he worked for them sincerely and faithfully.

Jagan had been attracted greatly by Ahmed Shah Masood's personality and skill in moving with people cordially. During the Soviet aggression, different groups worked in unison as friends against the common enemy, the Soviet Union. In 1989, the Soviet Union withdrew its troops completely from Afghanistan. The dummy government that was set up by Najibullah, who came to power, was able to survive only for a few years. The main reason for this was the disintegration of the Soviet Union, and the rise to power of Boris Yeltsin, who was against communism. He stopped totally, the supply of oil and arms. Najibullah did not have any other alternative than to leave Kabul and flee.

The irony of the matter is the fact that the Soviet Union, which attempted to make the whole world communist, finally broke into pieces itself! Afghanistan turned out to be a Waterloo not only for the Soviet Union. Later, like the bull attacking the very owner who reared it, when the Islamic militants attacked America, the latter's Afghan policy also met with failure.

Whatever the case may be, it was in April 1992, when Najibullah fell, that Jagan along with his friends reached Kabul.

They had established connections only with Ahmed Shah Masood, who belonged to the race that spoke the language called Tajik. It was the time, when Masood was manipulating things with the goal of ruling the northern parts of Afghanistan.

All the army units of the Mujahideen were proceeding rapidly towards Kabul; at the same time, talks regarding the Peshawar Treaty were going on. As General Dostum had left the Afghan army and joined Ahmed Shah Masood, the latter's strength had increased. When Masood gained control of Bagram airport 60 kms north of Kabul, he could have captured the whole of Kabul, had he wished so. But, the righteous man that he was, he wanted that all the warring factions should unite and establish a coalition government. Hence, he waited until he signed the Peshawar Treaty.

As for the warring factions, on one hand, they had involved themselves in the war along with Masood; on the other hand, they were intent on stabilizing their connections with their controllers in neighbouring countries like Pakistan, Saudi Arabia, Iran, and Uzbekistan. Thus, peace in Afghanistan became a mirage.

General Hekmatyar mistook Masood's patience for a weakness. He crossed the River

Kabul and engaged in missile attacks on Kabul city intermittently.

Although an interim government, which was a dummy one, was set up, the warring factions and their foreign financiers were more intent on augmenting and increasing their personal profits and power under the guise of peace. Rabbani and Hekmatyar assumed office as President and Prime Minister respectively. There was no understanding or unity between them.

It was at this juncture that Jagan came under the influence of Masood. He knew English fluently. In addition, he learnt to speak Urdu and Pashto.

Among the armies that attacked Kabul, it was to Ahmed Shah Masood's army, which came from the North that the air bases and the arms depots fell.

Moreover, since Masood was reputed for his magnanimity, the communist government armies and the officers surrendered to him and left Kabul.

At the same time, Hekmatyar's armies stationed in the South and West of Kabul were forced to retreat to their bases, though they managed to reach Kabul. Initially, Pakistan trusted Hekmatyar to achieve its goals. Gradually, as it realized that he was not a winning horse and that he had no influence over the people, it withdrew its support and assembled an organization called Taliban that was wholly under its control.

In the meantime, the Hezb e Islami, an organization belonging to Hekmatyar who had been driven out of Kabul, and the Iran-sponsored Hezb e Wahdat engaged in frequent missile attacks on Kabul.

An interim government headed by Rabbani was established. It had the support of Masood. However, they could not bring even the capital city of Kabul fully under their control. Important cities in other parts of the country, such as Kandahar and Jalalabad, fell into the hands of different armed gangs and were cut off. In the meanwhile, the situation became more complicated by the presence of Ittihad i Islami a group following the Wahaabi philosophy and promoted by Saudi Arabia.

During this period, General Rashid Dostum changed allegiance and joined hands with Hekmatyar. This affected the war conditions and forced Masood to retreat. Nevertheless, a staunch Masood recaptured his old bases.

It was under such chaotic conditions that the Taliban first appeared as an armed political organization. For the people who were dissatisfied with continual warfare, the Taliban seemed to promise a new dawn. Hence, it had the support of the people. From Kandahar city, the Taliban brought Southern Afghanistan under its control systematically.

With the support of Pakistan, Saudi Arabia, and Bin Laden's Al Qaeda, the Taliban captured Kabul in 1996, and established its rule. At that time, Masood moved Northwards with his army.

It was under these confused circumstances that Jagan came to them. As his fluency in English and skill in learning languages like Pashtun impressed his friends, he was given responsible jobs. His work included official talks, making strategic moves, communicating with service organizations and espionage agents, preparing reports, policy details, and propagandist materials and so on. In addition, he was also occasionally involved in patrol duty. Thus, they made full use of his services. Though he was able to meet foreign agents, he did not attempt to tell them anything about his condition. There were several reasons for this. First, he had embraced Islam only because of his genuine respect for that religion. The doctrine of equality advocated by that religion attracted him greatly. Moreover, he had been married to a lady chosen for him by Ahmed Shah Masood. She was older to him, and the widow of an army general who had been killed in the war. In addition to satisfying his physical needs, she had been taking care of him sincerely. Hence, his world had been circumscribed within that narrow limit, and he had lost the ability to think of anything outside that circle. Also, his bodyguards never allowed him to meet strangers alone.

Realizing that this was his life, he was engrossed in carrying out the duties allotted to him, as best as he could. He had truly changed himself to suit his Muslim name Jamaal. He did not attempt to think of anything other than that life. Neither did he have that capacity. This was because, every day he worked hard; when he went home, his wife attended to his needs, and then he slept off. The next day, once again he slogged like an ox yoked to an oilpress. He followed the ritual of worshipping five times a day. He experienced a kind of vacuum being drained of his strength, physically and mentally. He had no capacity to think.

The displacements resulting from the victories and defeats of war, the consequent changes, the time taken to get accustomed to these changes--life went on like this, mechanically.

He believed truly that he was contributing his share to Allah's war, and that on the Day of the Last Judgment he would attain eternal bliss.

It was during this time that an earthquake took place in his life suddenly.
While the Taliban captured Kabul, Masood's army units retreated into Northern Afghanistan. Although Jagan was not directly involved in the war, he was part of their army. Hence, he was made to stand in their midst. It was then that a series of missile attacks and explosions rocked Kabul. In this war, his wife died in front of his eyes, when a shell fell on her. In the confusion that ensued, he was caught by Pakistan's intelligence agency called the I.S.I, which had been helping the

I am the Lord

Taliban, and then handed over to the American C.I.A officials in a deal. Hundreds of people like him were imprisoned and interrogated by the C.I.A.

If the C.I.A were to take them to America, it could function only within the ambit of American laws. These laws did not allow physical or mental torture, indefinite detention and so on.

Because of this, men like Jagan were detained in secret camps in a third country. This practice is called rendering. The C.I.A adopted various techniques, such as spying on them, changing some of them into their own agents, and turning the others into intermediaries. Those who resisted were subjected to solitary confinement, waterboarding etc.

Jagan had been imprisoned in such a secret prison for the past one year. It is very difficult to change the minds of Islamic militants. Even if they were to be tortured beyond endurance limits, they would not deviate from their goal. No matter how many years they are imprisoned, once they are released many of them would return to their set goals.

It was under these conditions that Pastor Robert rendered yeoman service. The American prison authorities considered that Robert and his team were directing these militants to an alternative way of life.

When it was his turn to confess, Jagan narrated all these incidents openly without any reservations. He then felt as if he had unloaded a great burden from his mind. The others asked him several questions. In particular, they asked him about the people whom he met, Ahmed Shah Masood's policies, political philosophies, religious beliefs and so on.

Pastor Robert told him: "My son, you are like an open book. There should be no secrets in your mind. We belong to God's family. We have no secrets between us."

"After you have shared all your experiences, I shall pardon you and give you rebirth. After that, you can lead a new life."

"My son, Islam appeared several centuries after Christianity began. As far as we are concerned, God comprises the three entities of the Father, the Son, and the Holy Spirit. Islamists reject this concept. Also, they consider Jesus only as a messenger of God, not as God Himself. Apart from this, they refuse to accept the fact that the Bible is God's Word. The Last Judgment, indications of that, and the belief that Jesus will come again, are common to both religions.

"Only if you accept Jesus can you go to heaven; are you ready?"

"Yes, Pastor. I am ready to accept Jesus," said Jagan.

I am the Lord

"If you change your religion to prove your faith, are you willing to preach our religion and help to convert others also?" asked the Pastor.

"To the best of my ability I shall do everything to spread my new religion," said Jagan.

Ezhuth Aani

# 5

The specified day dawned. Having bathed and worn the new clothes given by the Pastor, Jagan went to the beach in Barceloneta. Many other prisoners like him had also been brought there. All their faces looked refreshed.

"Friends, you've all become ready for a new life. From today, you are going to be born anew. Henceforth, there will be prosperity in your life. If you prove yourselves to be good Christians and good citizens, I shall certainly get you your release," said the Pastor.

Following this, all of them prayed, immersed themselves in the sea, and rose. After Pastor Robert preached his sermon, just as they did one by one, Jagan too knelt, ate the bread, and drank the grape wine offered by the Pastor. The latter then placed his hand on Jagan's head.

Suddenly, he felt as if electricity or lightning struck him. "I give you the Holy Spirit. It will remain with you and lead you," said the Pastor and christened him John.

From that moment, Jagan felt strange sensations. He could not sleep for two days. It was as if an unknown power had entered his body and was directing him. It took him several days to recover gradually from that exalted state.

I am the Lord

Rapid changes took place in Jagan's life. The Pastor had him freed, and took him to cities like New York and Toronto. Later, he was put up in the Pastor's Bible College in Edmonton in Canada, and given intensive training.

The Pastor had told him not to communicate with outsiders, citing examples from the 2Corinthians 6:14, and Nehemiah's book. In the college, the Holy Bible was specially taught to him in Tamil. There were some others also with him. However, they evaded exchanging personal details of their lives with him.

The Pastor would often tell him: "God has given you a special duty. We have chosen you. We intend to settle you in the midst of the Tamils in Toronto, and establish a church for you in a place called Markham. But, before that you should stay for a year in the Nilgiris Mountains in Tamilnadu and help us to set up our churches there."

To go wherever the Pastor wanted him to go, to stay there, and establish churches, Jagan had no passport, visa, or monetary means. The Pastor had obtained a Canadian passport for him. As soon as the trip was over, he would take the passport with him. There was never a shortage of funds when he was with Pastor Robert, but he had no money of his own.

If a church was established in a place, its members would be asked to pay at least 10 per cent of their income to the Church. This was done in accordance with the religious laws called 'tithe', laid down by Apostle Paul. Apart from this, money flowed in from building funds, and the sale of books and food items. Huge sums also poured in from their headquarters. Importance was given to take 'the Good News' especially to countries like India, Africa, and China.

As Pastor Robert was engaged in changing the minds of the Islamic militants, huge sums of money came to him from somewhere. These Churches had been disconnected from a central control, and functioned as separate, autonomous units although strung together by a fine delicate thread. They were not subjected to any auditing or tax payment. They functioned only on the strong faith reposed in the Pastors concerned. Just as Moses led the Israelites, the Pastors led their devotees as God's agents.

Jagan was taught the traditions and customs of the communities of the Tamils in Tamilnadu, and the Sri Lankan Tamils in Toronto. He was given training in various tactics, such as how to visit temples dressed like Hindus in a veshti, kurta and turban, how to gauge the people there, how to identify and approach people who appear to be in distress, bogged down by problems in life, and how to gradually involve them in Bible reading and magnetize them towards Christ.

He was also taught the nuances of how, although we are part and parcel of society, like the shell and tamarind fruit, we should remain

I am the Lord

separate too. Our aim is to achieve our goal and focus on increasing our numbers. During social rituals and festivals or individual functions such as funerals or weddings, we should go invited or uninvited, and render help, and then spread the Good News, using the good reputation and respect acquired through this!

He was trained in charitable activities, such as rendering socially useful assistance, consoling the sick, and so on.

The Pastor would often say, 'Whatever good you do to others will be useless, unless you follow it up with the Lord's Good Word'.

Thus, only after rigorous training, Jagan was ready to face his new challenges.

# 6

**H**e was also taught how to handle Muslims. They have accepted many of the saints mentioned in the Old Testament as God's messengers. Along with Adam, Ibrahim (Abraham) and Moosa (Moses), they consider Jesus under the name of Esha also, as the Lord's messengers. Muslims too believe that on the Day of the Last Judgment, when the world is destroyed, Esha would come with fiery eyes riding a white horse. This belief concurs with what is said in the Revelation to John in the Bible. Moreover, they accept that the Gospels according to Mark, Matthew, John, and Luke are God's words, though distorted and revised. Jagan was taught how, initially he should stress on these similarities and win their confidence, then gradually persuade them as to why they should accept Christ, and then change their minds.

Islam emphasizes that there is but one God, Allah. Christianity worships the Trinity of the Father, the Son, and the Holy Spirit. Jagan was taught how Islamic doctrines have been misinterpreted — that women should be slaves, that they should not be educated, that men would be rewarded if they kill those who do not accept their policies — and how Christianity differs from this, and how he could use these facts to argue that Christianity is a better religion than Islam.

I am the Lord

Pastor Robert advised Jagan thus: "The weakness of Islam lies in its treatment of women. If only Muslim women are educated and acquire some knowledge of this world, they cannot be locked up in the illusion of ancient (conservative) traditions. How long can you imprison 50 per cent of the people in the darkness of ignorance? Hence, if you can organize conferences and work out employment schemes for women, and involve Muslim women in them, at least one or two women can be made to change their minds and embrace Christianity. Then, through them, the others too can be converted. If the women in a family are made to change their minds, gradually you can change the whole family."

"Similarly, when you approach the Hindus, you should introduce yourself to them, dressed like them very traditionally. By means of the story of Prajapathi, which occurs in the section called 'Purushasuktham' in the Rig Veda, you can turn them towards Christ. Prajapathi is immaculate; the other gods make him a scapegoat in their sacrificial fire. Prajapathi is described as a pure horse, which is tied to a pole, with a rope made of grass and cooked rice; the other gods make him out to be an unwanted creature and kill him. This can be compared to Jesus wearing a Crown of thorns and carrying a Cross, being taken to be sacrificed. Moreover, Prajapathi is depicted as one who silently bears all the torture inflicted on him. This too, can be compared to Jesus's patience; that is, if they accept that the coming of Jesus has already been mentioned in the Hindu Vedas, they will be more receptive. If they understand this, it will be easy for them to accept Jesus.

"Moreover, the story of Noah's Ark in the Bible is similar to that of the incarnation of Vishnu as a fish in the Vishnu Purana. The flood and King Sathyavradha's boat in this episode resemble the ones mentioned in the Bible.

"Like this, if you are able to connect the Hindu scriptures and convince the Hindus that the worship of Christ is not alien to Hindu culture, and make them accept it, you can easily change their minds.

"The experience that you acquire in India will be very useful to you in Toronto. The day is not far off when we shall bring all the Sri Lankan Tamils in Toronto into Christ's fold."

# PART III

# FREEDOM

# 1

Jagan returns to India in 1999. The same India, which he had left many years ago stealthily as an accused, as a fugitive, with militants as his companions, he now lands in legally as Father John, at the Indira Gandhi International airport. His Church had arranged his Canadian passport and Indian visa. Without any questioning and with great respect, he was allowed entry by the Immigration authorities. The Indian agents waiting for him, put him up at the Ashok Hotel for a day, and the next day saw him off to Coimbatore. There too, some members of his Church were waiting for him. From Coimbatore, they travelled for a few hours in an air-conditioned car past Mettupalayam, on the mountain road to the Nilgiris. There was no hitch in the program drawn up for him. On reaching the destination, one Father Leon was introduced to him.

Their Church was in a very pleasant place called Coonoor. In debates between creationists and evolutionists, the question that creationists ask is, "How can such a beautiful world and such wonderful plants and animals be created by evolution? Hence, they were created only by God." In this respect, Coonoor can be truly said to be a very charming creation of God.

The mountain ranges full of tea gardens appeared like a sea of green waves. Like the foam of the sea, fluffy balls of clouds rested on the mountaintops. Depending on the angle of sunlight falling, and the colour of the leaves, the various shades of green presented a beautiful picture as though created by an imaginative artist.

When one lives in such sylvan surroundings, how can one not think of Nature and its Creator? Their Church was surrounded by a huge garden. It was a new church built by the efforts of Father Leon. It was funded generously by foreign aid.

Apart from the church, there was a separate building complex nearby, consisting of hostels for the leaders and their assistants, a hall and so on.

There was a library also, with books related to Christianity. The kitchen was in another building. For procuring provisions, and for cooking, cleaning, washing etc., people from the neighbouring villages had been employed. They would come during the day, and return home after work. Jagan's life also went on smoothly. By means of their worship, preaching and propaganda, Jagan and his assistants acquired a considerable recognition in that society, and became indispensable members of that social structure.

Gradually, the number of people visiting their church increased. Those who came were given some work every day, and encouraged to join their group with their families. Thus, Leon and Jagan succeeded in bringing many families into their fold, like catching fish with some bait. Those who refused to bring in their families, found themselves separated and shattered. Thus, in that place, Jagan's and Leon's authority and respect kept increasing. In many families, all their decisions were taken only after consulting these Pastors. Even 80 year-olds waited for a word from these youths who were in their 20s. Whatever they said was accepted unquestioningly. Apart from this, offerings in the form of cash and kind poured in. From abroad too, they received funds. For the service of Jesus, everybody gave liberally. Construction work was begun for more buildings for their Church. More than this, they bought big houses that came up for sale in neighbouring towns, and established branches there. Leon's loyalists were employed to carry out the Lord's service in those branches. No accounts were maintained of their income or expenditure. Those who dared to ask questions were silenced by the argument that doubting God's agents was against the tenets of the Bible. It was at this juncture that Pastor Leon began pressurizing Jagan to marry his sister. Leon's sister was a widow, the mother of two children. When he asked for time to think over the matter, Jagan was given two weeks to decide. If he were to continue to remain with Leon, Jagan had to marry Matilda. Leon knew that after some time Jagan would be transferred to Canada. If the marriage were to take place before that, his sister and her children could go to Canada with Jagan; this was Leon's plan. In that case, he could be in charge of the Lord's 'kingdom' in Tamilnadu, while Jagan could be his counterpart in Canada. Thus, their family would have a bright future, thought Pastor Leon.

It was at this time that the Tamil New Year arrived. Leon wished to do something new in the New Year. He planned a campaign. Jagan and a few others were sent to Vellaiyangiri hills, dressed in the traditional Tamil manner, in a veshti, kurta, shawl, and turban. Vellaiyangiri was a cluster of seven hills in the southern part of the Western Ghats. The Hindus referred to it as Southern Kailash. There is a Sivan temple there, for Vellaiyangiri Andavar. The Hindus believed that the 'suyambu' (self-begotten) Siva lingam found in a natural cave at the top of a big hill among this cluster of hills near Poondi village, was a powerful form of Lord Siva. On both sides of the entrance to the cave, stand two tall boulders like Dwarapalakas (guards). Apart from this, natural springs, small hillocks and a sandy hill called Thiruneetrumalai, served to make the whole region a picturesque one. Leon had often thought, how wonderful it would be, if a branch of their Church could be set up there. If the members of his group, dressed like Hindus, could interact cordially with the Hindu devotees who would come there on New Year's Day, at least a few of them would accept the Gospel. Later, their branch could take root there gradually, and grow into a large tree; this was Leon's dream.

For this especially, Jagan along with five men and six women, all dressed in white, set up a small camp in the morning itself, at the foot of the

Vellaiyangiri hill, and offered water and food packets to the devotees coming there. A picture of Christ was also included. On the reverse of the picture, the following verse from John was printed. "For God sent not the Son into the world to judge the world; but that the world should be saved through him." For more details, they were asked to contact Leon's address and phone number. In addition, copies of the Bible were offered at lower prices to those who were interested in knowing more about the Bible, then and there.

Every day, their camp was open from five or six in the morning to ten in the night. They rested in turns. A friend of Pastor Leon had arranged their accommodation in Booluvampatti.

Leon had decided that the camp would be conducted for two weeks on an experimental basis, and if the people's response was good, it would be continued for some more time. He also planned that if Jagan agreed to marry his sister, the marriage too could be performed in that period.

Mother Nature had used all her skills to produce a wonder called the Nilgiris. Among the mountains, which comprised the Nilgiris, the Vellaiyangiri range appeared to be the most charming and luscious.

One should be fortunate to live in such serene surroundings. Thousands of people come here in search of spirituality, and the therapeutic value of the herbs and the air that caresses them. How

I am the Lord

lucky are the people who enjoy this sight and air daily, without the fatigue of a journey and at no cost? It was in such an ambience that Jagan and his team came, to expand their religious service eagerly.

Though Jagan had undertaken this journey happily, enthusiastically, and with great expectations, the deadline set by Pastor Leon kept pricking him in a corner of his mind. He had to announce his decision at the end of these two weeks. Leon's sister was beautiful, of course! Nevertheless, he had his own doubts as to whether there was any compatibility between them, physically, mentally and intellectually, for him to be able to spend the rest of his life with her. He had the experience of having been almost forcibly married in Afghanistan. He doubted whether at his age, he was capable of shouldering the responsibility of taking care of a lady with two young children. Although he realized that in the service of God, individual sacrifices had to be made, he could not believe fully that this plan would give long-term happiness to both the parties concerned. At the same time, he knew only too well that if he refused to accept Pastor Leon's proposal, he could not continue to remain there for long.

When he thought of where he would go if he left that place, an unknown fear seized him. If he stepped out of the circle of the service of God, he did not know what his next step could be. Once he had surrendered to the Family of God, he had no necessity to take independent decisions. Others decided everything for him. For the first time now, he was under compulsion to take a decision. The fact that his decision would affect not only himself but also many others scared him greatly. Every time he thought about it, his forehead perspired and his heart raced in agitation. Hence, he relegated this problem to a corner of his brain, and concentrated on carrying out his daily duties. The decision to be taken, hung over his head like Damocles' sword.

Under such circumstances, Jagan focused his mind on spending each new day for its own sake. Whether Hindus or Christians, hunger and thirst are common to all, is it not? From the behaviour of the people who came there, Jagan understood that hunger can drive one to any extremes, and that when one gives water to the thirsty the receiver will always be grateful to the giver. Jagan and his team desisted from giving non-vegetarian food to the people who came. Some of them gave their phone numbers and addresses. Some bought copies of the Bible. Every day, many of them showed an interest in the Gospel. When Salvation and Absolution are offered free like food and water, would anyone refuse to receive them?

One day, when he was engrossed in his daily routine, he heard that voice. "You say that the Lord sent His Son only to save us, and not to judge us. In the same Gospel of John chapter 9, Jesus says, "And Jesus said, "For judgment I came into this world, so that those who do not see may see, and that those who see may become blind." (John 9:39)

I am the Lord

When he heard those words, in pure Tamil but with a different accent, a bell rang in Jagan's mind. Yes. It was a very familiar voice! That too, a voice which he loved ever so deeply once upon a time.

Jagan turned in the direction from where the voice had come. There ... He could not believe what he was seeing! Yes. His ex-dream girl, the goddess of beauty, was looking at him with a smile.

A very fair body, blond hair plaited tight. Her blue eyes shone like stars. Clad like a typical Indian girl in a sandal wood coloured sari and a red blouse, with a vermillion dot on her forehead, she stood like a queen. Once upon a time, she was the Queen of his heart.

"Olivia!" cried Jagan, in a voice that combined surprise and disbelief.

The response was in the same tone. "Jagan!"

"How come here?"

"I'm asking the same."

The others, who had come with Jagan, surrounded them. He introduced Olivia to them as a long-standing friend.

Later, when they were having lunch, Olivia said, "You have not answered my question yet."

Ezhuth Aani

"You should not take the verses in the Bible in isolation. Every verse must be considered, taking into account the situation in which it was uttered," said Jagan.

"In that case, don't you believe that every word in the Bible came from the Lord?" asked Olivia again.

"I fully believe it. The Bible was written directly by the Lord or said to man indirectly through inspired saints," said Jagan.

"The two verses mentioned by you were both written by St. John. There is a great contradiction between the two. How can you justify that?" asked Olivia.

Jagan's team members, unable to make out who it was who questioned their leader thus in the singular, watched both of them very uneasily.

"How did you learn Tamil? And how did you come here?" asked Jagan.

"How did you become a Christian Pastor?" asked Olivia.

The manner in which she questioned him on an equal level, was a new experience for him. Ever since he had converted to Christianity, he had only seen people nodding in approval of what the leaders said; he had never experienced being cornered with questions. Olivia's action did not annoy him. On the other hand, on seeing her big rolling eyes and rosy lips when she spoke, his old memories flooded his mind. He wanted to hug her tightly. His social status and the others' presence restrained him from doing any such thing.

During the next few days, Olivia spent most of her time with them. Jagan struggled, unable to answer her questions. He could not explain why they were staying in a different place, when Karunya Nagar, established by Bro. Dinakaran was close to their camp. The fact was that Pastor Leon was more interested in expanding his Church, rather than spreading Christianity with the help and co-operation of Bro. Dinakaran.

Every small division (of the Christian Church) believed that **it** was the only true follower of Christ and that the others were false and heretics. It was customary for them to choose any verse from the Bible, project it as an important tenet of Christianity, say that the others did not follow it, and hence they should be rejected. According to this, there are differences between the various Christian divisions, with respect to their dietary habits, acceptance of blood transfusion, administering medicines for ailments and one's dress and behaviour in general. Even for baptism, some consider immersion in water as important. Others say that it is not necessary. However, every group believed that it alone would go to Heaven. Thus, Pastor Leon wanted to avoid going Dinakaran's way, and preferred to take his own path. Hence, Leon's team desisted from going to

Karunya Nagar and getting any help from that group.

As Jagan recounted his experiences, Olivia too described the events that took place in her life during the past few years.

They were classmates in school. They were inseparable friends then.

When a person is able to share what is in his mind with another without any expectation or hesitation, the two become true friends. Such a friendship does not exist even between many married couples. Several husbands do not reveal all their innermost thoughts and feelings to their partners. This is because of the fear that if they disclose what is in their mind, it might produce adverse reactions.

In this respect, Olivia and Jagan were true friends. Though they had not indulged in sex freely, they were quite intimate in many ways. They had intended to get married after their studies. It was then that Jagan went to India, and was lost.

When Jagan did not return, all kinds of rumours were afloat. In Australia, it was rumoured that Jagan belonged to the Liberation Tigers, that he was a member of the suicide bomb squad, and that in the explosion that killed Rajiv Gandhi, he too had been killed. Some said that Jagan went to Sri Lanka along with the Liberation Tigers.

I am the Lord

Jagan's family almost concluded that he had died, and functioned accordingly. Every year, on the day Rajiv was murdered, Jagan's parents observed his death anniversary.

Olivia was a Greek by lineage; her parents were Catholics. She too followed the same religion from childhood.

When Jagan was lost, there was a huge void in her life. Her mind refused to accept that Jagan was dead. At that time, she did not have the strength, knowledge, or financial power to investigate this matter. However, she decided that her long-term goal in life was to somehow go to India, and engage herself personally in investigating his whereabouts.

With this aim, she excelled in her school studies, and winning a scholarship went to Harvard University. There, along with Economics and South Asian Studies, she chose Tamil as a subject. When she was in America, she got involved in Satguru Jaggi Vasudev's Isha Foundation. Later, for her post-graduation she came to Madras University, and visited all the places that Jagan had visited, trying to gather some clues about him. All the clues disappeared with the day on which Rajiv Gandhi was killed.

During this period, although some relationships were formed, she did not feel committed to them deeply. As far as she was concerned, her first and true lover was Jagan. Even if she tried to forget him, she could not. It was at this time that she became greatly involved in the activities of the Isha Foundation. The deeper she became involved in the Isha Foundation the more clearly she realized that it was also like the other organizations. If men found a charismatic leader and had unquestioning faith in him, they can be led around like sheep and cattle. Thus disillusioned, she had begun to dissociate herself from the Isha magic, but she paid periodic visits to their meditation centre near the Vellaiyangiri hills. The natural beauty of the place and the peace prevailing there, were a source of great solace to her. Whether everything that the Satguru said was true or not, one thing that he had said had come true. That is, if we were to focus our whole mind on one particular desire, our wishes would be fulfilled and the desire will come to fruition. She was very happy at the thought that this unexpected meeting with Jagan was the fruit of all her efforts of the past so many years.

Although she was not against Christianity, she decided that if she were to stir and wake Jagan up from his delusions, she must make him think independently, by challenging his doctrines and philosophies.

Jagan also confessed all his experiences without any reservations. He told her about the enforced wedding, which took place in Afghanistan. However, he tried to bring her round to his path. He told her that the Bible was the Lord's Word, that one could find answers to all the questions of life in the Bible, and that only when one read it devoutly, one could find its true message. He also said that it was because some Christian groups distanced themselves from the Holy Bible, that they indulged in activities contrary to the true path of Christianity.

"Look at this beautiful world. How many types of plants and animals are there? Look at the Sun! Look at the Moon! Look at the stars! Were they self-created? Without a Creator, how did they appear?" asked Jagan, looking at her closely.

"Don't you believe in evolution? If as you claim, all that is said in the Bible is absolutely true, is the world only 6000 years old?" asked Olivia.

Silence prevailed for some time.

Breaking it herself, she said, "We often quote from John's Gospel, chapter 14, verse 6, which says, 'Jesus saith unto him, I am the way, and the truth, and the life: no one cometh unto the Father, but by me.' In this, what is the true meaning of 'I'? Does it not refer to the Brahman, or the Ultimate Reality which is within all of us?"

"Jesus Christ spoke in the Aramaic language. This was later translated into Greek, Latin, Hebrew, and finally, English. Even in English, there are several translations. Such being the case, how can you say that every word in the Bible is the absolute Truth? Depending on the reader's maturity, the meaning can change, is it not? As far as I am concerned, the "I" which He used refers to the Supreme Soul. In the book Exodus, God says that "I" refers to Him, the Supreme Soul. Hence, my view is that everything is within us. This is what Jesus meant when He said, "neither shall they say, Lo, here! or, There! for lo, the kingdom of God is within you. Luke (17:21). "Among the four Gospels, the one written by Mark is the first. Many scholars acknowledge that this was written in the 60s or 70s CE.; that is, thirty to forty years after the death of Christ. The gospels of Luke and Matthew have certain parts reproduced from that of Mark. John's gospel has some sections taken from Luke's. Despite this, in the matter of Christ's lineage, Matthew and Luke contradict each other.

"Mark and Luke did not live with Jesus as His Apostles. At the same time, the gospel written by Thomas who was an Apostle of Christ, has been left out of the Bible.

"A part of Thomas's gospel says: 'I am the Omnipresent Light; I am everything; everything is born out of me and everything will return to me. If you split a tree, I will be there. If you move a stone, you can see me there also'. These verses describe the doctrine of Advaita closely. Unfortunately, the writings of Thomas who had been with Christ have been excluded.

"Moreover, as I said earlier, Matthew's and John's writings are based on Mark's book. In other words, why should Matthew and John, who are apostles, follow what was written by Mark who was not an apostle?

I am the Lord

"Several books were collected and compiled into one book around 400 CE; it was the final edition, the canonisation of the Bible, and the Bible consisted of 66 books. Even in these, some differences exist between the Bibles followed by the Catholics and the Protestants. There are some additional sections in the Catholics' Bible. Moreover, books like Judith and Maccabees are accepted by the Catholics, but not by the Protestants. Similarly, Eastern Churches like the Greek Orthodox Church accept certain books, which are not accepted by the Western Churches.

"Martin Luther, a religious reformist, had said that books like Hebrews, James, Jude, and Revelation must be removed from the Bible, as they contained things that were not consistent with the other books.

"How can such confusion prevail in the book which you claim is God's Word? It was man who determined which book should be included in which order, and which should be discarded.

"If you read it carefully, you will realize that there are several contradictions in this book. I have not come to list them. I shall tell you a few of them.

"Jesus Christ taught us unconditional love. I respect and admire that. According to the Old Testament, the Lord is said to have instigated Joshua to carry out ethnic cleansing of His enemies. How can Jesus Christ who advocated, 'If a man strikes you on one cheek, show him the

Ezhuth Aani

other', endorse genocide? It was with such contradictions that it was possible to justify the Crusade Wars and the racial cleansing that was carried out in South America.

"Next, I wish to tell you something else. According to Luke's Gospel chapters 9 and 21, Jesus had foretold that the world would end before the generation that existed then, died. Even after 2000 years, that has not happened. In the meantime, so many men predicted that the world would end, and extorted money by cheating people.

"In Australia, hundreds of people believed Rev. Moon's prediction, sold their houses, and taking only the essentials, prepared themselves for their journey. They did it only because they feared that the world would end on a particular day.

Paul played a major role in linking the Old Testament, which is the history of the Jews, with the story of Jesus Christ, and presenting it as a message to the whole world. His main philosophical tenets were the First Sin and Atonement," said Olivia, reeling out detailed explanations very casually.

Interrupting, Jagan said, "All men are born as sinners. The only path of redemption lies in accepting the fact that Jesus Christ sacrificed Himself as atonement for us, is it not?"

Olivia replied to this question thus, "If you want I can cite a hundred verses from the Bible itself to show that children are not born as sinners. Without wasting your time, I shall quote just a few examples. In the 18th and 18th chapters of Matthew, Christ says clearly: "Verily I say unto you, Except ye turn, and become as little children, ye shall in no wise enter into the kingdom of heaven." and "But Jesus said, Suffer the little children, and forbid them not, to come unto me: for to such belongeth the kingdom of heaven." that is, He considered children as innocent, not as sinners. The same idea is found in the 10th chapter of Mark, and the 18th chapter of Luke's Gospel. Similarly, in the very first chapter of the Bible and many other books, God is said to have created Man in His likeness. How can the flawless Lord create sinful creatures? There are several other examples.

Paul first put forward the doctrine of atonement. In the religion of the Jews, the practice of sacrificing animals to atone for one's sins had been followed traditionally from ancient times. It is but natural for men with such an attitude, to substitute animals with men. Taking two verses from Mark, St. Paul has expanded them from the first epistle written to the Thessalonians, to the first epistle written to the Corinthians and that written to the Romans. However, this doctrine of atonement was not widespread among the Christians living then. In his book James has said, "Even so faith, if it have not works, is dead in itself." (James 2:17) According to Paul, accepting just the concept of the Lord's atonement is sufficient for one's Salvation. Thus, if you read history, you can understand clearly how the ideas regarding the importance of Christ's sacrifice have been defined systematically, to form the basis of the beliefs of the modern, neo-Christians.

"Thomas Jefferson, one of the pioneers of American independence, and intellectuals like George Bernard Shaw were of the opinion that St. Paul revised Christ's teachings. Ancient followers of Christ called Essene Christians believed that Paul was a Roman spy. Paul also side-lined Christ's own brother, James. Paul changed Christ's teaching of unconditional love into conditional love. That is, Paul imposed upon Christians the condition that they could engage themselves in relationships like marriage, only with those who were Christians by religion. Similarly, in his Epistles, Paul laid stress on views that were meant to enslave women, such as that they should be subordinate to men, and that they should not speak in churches and so on. In the same vein, he denounced homosexuals as sinners. This is mentioned clearly in Romans (chapter 1), 1 Corinthians (chapter 6) and 1 Timothy (chapter 1), among others.

"Moreover, in many places Paul supports the idea of one man being a slave to another. He has also said in his books like Timothy and Hebrews, that one should be faithful to one's master. These words of his helped to justify the slave trade and for racial organizations like the Ku-Klux-Klan to

I am the Lord

consider the superiority of the Whites as a Biblical truth.

"If you say that God created Man in His own image, how can you accept the presence of slaves?

"If you say that only those who accept Jesus as the Lord will go to Heaven, what is your answer to this? If you count the number of people who have passed in this world and those who are now living, it would exceed a hundred billion. In today's world, only one third of the population is Christian. Even in that, there are hundreds of sub-divisions. According to you, Dinakaran's followers are on the wrong path; only your group will go to Heaven. It is 200,000 years since Man appeared in this world. That is, a majority of these hundred billion people lived and died before Christ. Even after Christ, how many centuries have passed before Christianity spread to Europe? Subsequently, the Europeans spread Christianity as an instrument of their imperialistic expansion, only within the last 600 years. Until then, in the Asian and American continents, and Oceania, which includes Australia and other pacific islands, Jesus Christ was not known at all. Even after so many years, only one out of three people say that they are Christians. Even among these, the majority do not follow Christ's teachings in their lives.

"If what you say is true, more than ninety per cent of the people will go to Hell. Moreover, you consider only human beings as living creatures. As far as I am concerned, animals and plants are also living creatures; in fact, even bacteria and viruses. In that case, do they not have a Judgment or Salvation? That is, in a newly risen world, will there be plants and animals? Dinosaurs? As mentioned earlier, when the majority of men are toiling in hell, and with no judgment for animals, if all the creatures, which have died so far, were to be resurrected, won't it be rare to find Man in heaven? Indeed, man will be a rarity in heaven! Just reflect on that.

"Consider this also. Do you think that in this vast Universe, there are living creatures only on earth? How do you know that there are no planets like the earth that contain life forms, surrounding the other stars?

"Have you read the book, 'Autobiography of a Yogi'? In it, Paramahamsa Yogananda explains the knowledge, which he obtained through yoga. He also describes the various conditions of existence. In this Universe, our Earth is a small negligible part. That being the case, who is going to save the creatures on the other planets?" asked Olivia, after her long discourse.

"In Hinduism, they say that the Soul does not die. In that case, how does the world's population increase? It should have been static from the time of creation," asked Jagan, interrupting. He thought he had beaten Olivia in her own game.

"A good question. At least now, I believe you have begun thinking independently," said Olivia smiling.

"This is a question which Pastor Leon asks the Hindus," said Jagan.

"Ha, ha! This too had to be taught by the pastor, is it?" said Olivia, laughing aloud.

"I'm not a Hindu. According to the Hindus' belief, there is a Supreme Soul called Brahman in each one of us. It is there in both living and nonliving things. The Brahman can shrink itself into one entity or multiply itself into many billions of forms. That is why, once upon a time, there were only dinosaurs and other ancient creatures in this world. That state can recur. The Brahman does not perish. This is compatible with the modern scientific theories about the origin of the Universe.

"You, that is, the Evangelicals, follow the Bhakti yoga; that is, selecting an object worthy of worship, then bestowing unlimited love on it, and through that love realizing oneself. St. Paul preached that this was the only path of realizing God. But, Jesus's brother James stressed the importance of good deeds. His doctrine is similar to the Karma yoga advocated by the Hindus. It implies doing one's duties without any expectations.

"Apart from this, Thomas, one of the Apostles of Jesus, said that one could realize oneself through reflection. The Hindus call realizing oneself through meditation and reflection Gnana yoga. This is what the Buddha followed.

"Thus, we can see various Hindu doctrines in Jesus Christ's teachings. In other words, unlike men who have eyes but see not, we can understand all this if we rationalize all that we see.

"In the Bhagavad Gita, Lord Krishna has said, 'I am the first of all letters'. The Tamil poet Thiruvalluvar also says the same thing. 'A' leads the alphabets; the Lord Almighty Leads and lords over the entire world. In the Revelation of the New Testament, the Lord says the same as, 'I am the Alpha and the Omega'.

"Consider well, Jagan. All religions preach the same thing. It is man who differentiates and rules by dividing the people. If life is a straight line, where will it end? Everlasting Kingdom, you say. If life is eternally in the same state, it will soon become tedious and boring. No, no. Life is a cycle. A cycle has no beginning and no end. Birth and death are two aspects of the same point. If you realize this, 'you know yourself'".

"Have you become a Hindu then?" asked Jagan in a hurried tone.

"Not at all. I was born a Christian! I shall die a Christian. My upbringing, culture and so on, are all

I am the Lord

based on Christianity. My roots and props are also based on Christianity. I shall never change my religion. Nor is there any need for it. But, I strive to understand other religions and the people who follow them. Everyone is taught certain views strongly in childhood. They are the anchors that help men from being washed away by the ocean of life. They are the roots, which save one from falling, when a storm called destiny blows over a man. Even if the branches break and fall, if the roots are firm, they will help the branches to grow again and prosper.

"You were born a Hindu. You are deep-rooted in Hindu culture. When I see you leaving your roots and following other religions, I am pained.

"Do you know about the world famous Curtain Fig tree in a place called Yungaburra? Do you know how it originated? The seeds dropped by birds on the original tree, began growing on its branches, and later to sustain themselves, they let down subsidiary roots, which we call prop roots. Thus, many prop roots grow down from the tall branches in every direction towards the ground, surround the mother tree, suffocating and strangling it so much that it dies, being deprived of nourishment and water. In other words, the seeds that began life as parasites have now grown into a huge tree. The tree that offered food, sustenance, and shelter for these seeds to grow, sacrificing itself to become a skeleton, died prematurely. What do you understand from this? If you allow alien roots to grow on you and cut off your own roots, you will meet with the same fate as that tree! One's roots are very important for everyone. When you lose your roots, you become a zombie or a corpse," she cautioned.

"It has been found that the same changes occur in the functioning of the brains of Tibetan monks involved in meditation, and the Catholic nuns when they engage in prayer. It is the hippocampus, a part of our brain that controls our beliefs regarding religion. It is believed that changes occur in this part. The same changes occur whether you meditate on Jesus, Allah, or Krishna.

"Why should the true incidents happening in your life, which you consider as miracles, not be the result of the changes taking place in your brain? In other words, why did it not strike you that your feelings are not real but illusions produced by certain chemical reactions taking place in your brain?" she asked, and waited for his answer.

Jagan's response was the question, "What do you think of Daniel's predictions?"

"What is the proof that your so-called prophesies of Daniel were written by Daniel himself? On the contrary, they may have been written after the events took place, mayn't they? This is exactly what the Greek philosopher Porphyry, who lived in the 3$^{rd}$ century A.D, asked. Even if we accept that Daniel wrote all this in 500 B.C, there have been greater empires in this world, than the four great empires of Babylonia, Persia, Greece, and Rome. Again, accepting that the Chinese and Incan empires did not sustain in the Middle East, have you forgotten that the Ottoman and Mongolian empires dominated several regions including the Middle East? Moreover, did not the imperialistic governments of Britain, America, France, Spain, Portugal, and Italy control several parts of the world? Did not the Soviet Union, Nazi Germany and Japan rule many parts of the world? Can we say that all these descended from the Roman Empire? Hence, those who consider Daniel's prophesies to be true are trying to interpret all the incidents within the limits of their doctrines. Those who view this neutrally and objectively will understand the truth.

"In the ancient world, there was a Greek robber called Procrustes. He would tie those whom he captured during the course of his robbery, to his cot. He would then cut off the legs of those who were taller than him, to fit the size of the cot. Similarly, he would tie ropes to the necks and legs of those shorter than him, and pull them from both ends to fit the length of the cot. Thus, those who tailor information to suit their needs are committing the error of Procrustes.

"You say that every single word in the Bible is the Truth. Have you read the book Ecclesiastes, which is part of the Old Testament? The doctrines mentioned in it are very similar to those of Jean Paul Sartre's existentialism. If this is also considered as the Lord's Word, is it not contrary to the other Scriptural teachings?"

Jagan interrupted her asking, "Being a Christian, can you talk ill of the Bible thus?"

"I am a Christian. I was born a Christian. You belong to a religious cult that brainwashes. These cults are parasites that suck up "the body, the assets, and the soul" of their members and deprive them of their capacity to think for themselves. First, they shower their love and win your confidence. Then, under the guise of a confession, they will make you share all your personal matters with them openly. When a man's personal secrets are made public, the boundaries of his identity disappear. After that, he becomes a faceless, nameless entity. His life is shaped by his leader's likes and dislikes. Subsequently, his individual freedom, desires, and efforts cease to exist. Your control over your life is removed from you and taken over by somebody else.

"A program will be drawn up for you, consisting of jobs that are of no use to you, and responsibilities that take up all your time. For example, every day there will be some work or the other, such as reading the Scriptures, sale of books, music practice and so on. Because of this, you will have no time to be with your family or friends. If you are caught in this wheel like a hamster, your body, and mind will become very fatigued, due to your hectic schedules. Gradually, you will lose your capacity to think independently. Even in doing your daily chores and dealing with small minor things you will have to seek the advice of the pastor. We cannot say that this practice exists only in Christian groups. Such destructive practices are found in some Hindu, Muslim, and even political organizations.

"These organizations will never acknowledge that they nurture such groups. I was involved in the Isha Foundation. I realized later that it was not entirely dissimilar to this. The leaders of cults will keep you in an entranced state by using methods like hypnotism. Only when you release yourself from that illusion, will you realize how they had turned your mind and soul into sedge grass or an empty bag. When you understand the reality, you will feel terribly frustrated and agonized at having been deceived.

"Many people realize that they are being deceived. Having been accustomed to allowing others to take decisions on their behalf, they are scared to step out of that circle. Frightened of the consequences, they remain imprisoned in the extreme religiosity of their own making.

"Do you know what the Stockholm syndrome is? In a bank robbery that took place in the Swedish capital of Stockholm, some of the bank employees were kept as hostages for five days. Even after the hostage drama ended, some of the hostages supported the robbers, and rejected the assistance of the government officials. Thus, the attitude of liking those who exploited us physically and mentally is called the Stockholm syndrome. Similarly, members of these religious groups begin to love those who use them. Some become slaves of the feelings of guilt and shame, arising out of the public confession of their sins. Being disgraced by the confession of the sins committed physically or mentally, becomes more or less an opiate for them." Jagan was in a confused state, understanding but trying not to understand the points detailed by Olivia.

"OK, OK; why don't you talk something else?" pleaded Jagan.

They then spoke about their school days, former relationships, and families for a long time.

Olivia had been in contact with Jagan's sister from those very days. Hence, she was well aware of the trauma his family had gone through after he got lost.

In talking to her for many hours, Jagan began to slacken in his work. Without his former enthusiasm in spreading the Word of Christ, he started his every day work anticipating the arrival of Olivia. The others did not fail to observe the change in his behaviour. Immediately the news was conveyed to Pastor Leon. In a couple of days, as expected, orders were received from Pastor Leon for Jagan to return to the Church at Coonoor. He was disappointed and sad.

I am the Lord

During the few days that he interacted with Olivia once again, both of them simultaneously felt as if they had not been separated all these years. They also realized that their love was deep and sincere.

It was imperative that he should return to Coonoor the next morning. He had been summoned. In the evening, after work was over, Jagan sent the others away and waited for Olivia.

# 2

It was a full moon night. The whole area was drenched in the milk-white moonlight. There was not a single cloud in the sky. The stars decorated the sky like flowers strewn all over. Having completed their pilgrimage, people were descending from the hills. Only Jagan and Olivia were climbing. In the moonlight, the mountain springs and ponds shone like silver plates. The splashing of the springs and cascades sounded like the bells of the anklets on the dancing feet of Mother Nature. The sounds of the wild animals in the distance reminded them that danger was not far away.

Suddenly, Olivia asked, "If a bear or an elephant were to appear now, will you save me?"

"Even at the cost of my life, I will," said Jagan with manly determination. Both of them had long sticks and torchlights in their hands. Bags containing food and water hung on their shoulders.

As time passed, the movement of people reduced and then vanished altogether. It was as if Time stood still. Both of them had lost themselves in each other. They talked about all kinds of things. Apparently, they had decided that they would somehow prolong the night, in view of the fact that at dawn the next day they would have to separate.

I am the Lord

It was then that it happened. Quite naturally, without any planning, and as a continuation of their friendship. The arms that had embraced each other as an indication of their support tightened their grip unwilling to separate. The kiss, which originated at the top of the head, blossomed on the lips. The tongues that had been talking all this while now began to sing silently. In the heat of their bodies, their dresses took leave of them. Their forms adhered to each other like a mould and its cast. In the frenzied dance of Nature, one form entered the other. With the bare ground for a bed and the star-studded sky as a blanket, the drama of physical union unfolded in the open. The earth gaped open, trembled and the flood receded. Was this the Apocalypse? Two lives died and were resurrected. Is this not a play of Nature? Is there a distinction of colour for this? A distinction of religion? In trying to make the other happy, each derived happiness. Though this was not the first time that they had had sex, this was a new experience. When the body, the mind and the spirit all unite, is there a match for it? That they had been friends since childhood was a different thing. That they had loved each other was also a different matter. Now, the two had become one – the blissful state of the Supreme Soul!

Having spent the whole night without sleep, and experienced the intoxication of a physical union, both of them prayed that the next day should not dawn. Just as Savithri had steeped the Sun in darkness to save her husband, Sathyavaan, just as the Goddess transformed a new moon night

Ezhuth Aani

into a full moon night to save the life of Abhiramipattar, Jagan, and Olivia longed that the laws of nature be stalled and the night should not end in sunrise.

In reality, the night passed and the Sun rose. They were compelled to face the harsh truths of life. They washed themselves in the waterfall and got dressed. They were depressed at the thought that soon they would have to take leave of each other.

"Why can't you come with me? We can go somewhere and live together," said Olivia.

"I am in a responsible position. Several souls are waiting for redemption through me. Forgive me," said Jagan, with a heavy heart.

He then took down her mobile phone number, and with the assurance that somehow, he would contact her later, he bid her farewell.

Olivia returned to Chennai.

After having experienced the height of bliss the previous night, Jagan's mind plunged into the abyss of sadness the next day. Exhausted with climbing the hill, scaling the peak of emotions, and spending a sleepless night, Jagan somehow managed to reach Coonoor and went to meet Pastor Leon.

I am the Lord

After making him wait for an hour, Pastor Leon met him. He appeared to be furious. Walking up and down, and then across the room for some time in silence, he asked, "Where is that white whore?"

"There's no need to address her disrespectfully like that," said Jagan.

"Oh! Has just one night's sexual pleasure caused you to develop such respect for her? How many plans I had made for you! If you had married my sister, we would have built a strong Church here. How have you shattered everything for the sake of a petty, transient joy?" said Pastor Leon, and losing his patience, he slapped Jagan. As the latter did not show any resentment, he slapped him on the other cheek also.

"From today, I divest you of all your responsibilities temporarily. Next Sunday, you should confess all your sins in detail in the presence of everybody openly ... You may go now" he said, and sent him off.

Returning to his room, Jagan squirmed in disgrace. His feeling of shame seemed to consume him. He asked himself why he lost his ethics thus. At the same time, he wondered what was wrong in a man and a woman loving each other and uniting! Who gave Pastor Leon the authority to judge or chastise them? His mind kept asking these questions repeatedly. If he were to confess his 'wrongs,' it would be a violation not only of his privacy, but also Olivia's. His inner self told him that it was wrong.

Having spent the whole night tossing and turning sleeplessly, the next morning Jagan went to the post office and got in touch with Olivia through STD. On hearing her voice, he was infused with a new courage and enthusiasm. He told her all that had taken place.

"Leave that group immediately," she said.

"Leave and go where? What shall I do?"

Though all his needs had been taken care of, he had no money of his own.

Leon had arranged everything. Hence, he hesitated.

Understanding his hesitation, Olivia said, "You are a prisoner of your faith. Do you understand at least now that you are in a gold-plated prison? I am a slave only to love. You are a slave in the circle, which you have circumscribed for yourself. You are scared about what there is outside that circle. There are many like you. Even after the veil of illusion is removed, they are afraid and hence, keep going round and round within that circle. Be bold and step out.

"Your experiences are unusual. You may not have a university degree. The school of life has taught you some rare lessons. Material possessions

I am the Lord

and assets will be yours today, but they may disappear tomorrow. Your wealth is in your brain. Whatever you do, if you involve yourself fully you'll certainly succeed.

"I knew that if you leave your prison you won't have any money with you. That is why I have left some money in Indian currency and a few Australian dollars with my friend Ravi, who is in the Isha Foundation near Vellaiyangiri. If you contact him somehow, he will help you," said Olivia encouragingly.

Even his passport was with Leon. He knew very well that in this struggle, he was David and Leon was Goliath.

Leon knew his entire past, including his escape from the Indian prison. Pastor Leon had friends all over India. If he were to be caught again, he would be at the mercy of people like Gupta in an Indian prison and experience...

The very thought made him shudder. At the same time, he thought if he were to surrender to Leon again, how his life would be. Golden handcuffs! He would be a parrot in a beautiful cage. For its daily food, the parrot would have to repeat the words of its master. It cannot fly with the other birds freely and make the sounds of its choice, in the rhythm of its choice. Of course, animals may attack the parrots flying outside. Better to die breathing the air of freedom, than suffer imprisonment in the name of security.

Ezhuth Aani

As far as Olivia was concerned, she needed him but not as a rootless tree. Not as a fully brainwashed zombie. She wanted a freethinking man. She wanted him to be a full man, one who understood himself fully, and one who was confident. She had rejected several groups, which functioned forgetting the important teachings of Jesus Christ, such as 'the Sermon on the Mount'.

The time had come for Jagan to take a crucial decision in his life. He had to choose between the life of a slave with safety, pleasure, and an assured future, and a new life full of freedom and an autonomous joy but an uncertain future. Though he chose the second option, his brain kept creating an unknown fear in him.

Finally, Jagan decided. Without even a change of dress, he took different modes of transport and reached the Isha Meditation Centre. There, a man called Ravi gave him refuge for two days. By then, members of Leon's group came searching for him. Those who leave such groups are called 'backsliders'. Backsliders were looked down upon as worse than sinners. Sinners can be redeemed. But, people like Leon knew that if the backsliders are not brought back under their control, either by isolating them or by using other threats and coercion, it would be a great challenge to their authority, although it was their view that it was very difficult to reclaim one who had already been redeemed once, but had slid back. If the backsliders were allowed to have their own way, they would be setting a very bad example to many

I am the Lord

who had doubts in their faith, but had not left the group out of fear. This was the belief of men like Leon: if many were to leave the group, thus there would be no discipline in the organization, which might disappear altogether in course of time.

Jagan had crossed the limit. Hence, taking him again into the fold and getting his sister married to him, was out of the question. Leon began to look at him as an enemy. It was his malicious intention that either Jagan should be brought back and punished, or using his contacts, he should be imprisoned or eliminated in some other way. He resolved firmly that Jagan's fate must be shown as an example to the others. There are several ways to punish those who betrayed their Church. They could be ostracized in society as untouchables. Or they could be subjected to various mishaps, which could be represented as God's punishment. If such people suffered from some disease or misfortune, it could be made to appear as an act of God in their propaganda, which would make the victim experience hell on earth.

When his group members came searching for Jagan, Ravi diverted them with great presence of mind and made them believe that Jagan was not there.

Jagan did not have his Canadian passport. It was with Leon. Moreover, it had his photograph but not his real name. It was a fake passport taken in someone else's name. Without any identification document, he could not leave India. The Australian

Embassy in India was in Delhi. If he were to travel to Delhi under the present circumstances, there was every possibility of his being caught by the Indian police or by Leon's friends. Wondering if there was any other way of leaving India, Jagan was terribly confused.

Moreover, Leon knew that Olivia had gone to Chennai. If he were to go there immediately, he was sure to fall under Leon's observation.

Hence, Jagan decided that he would first go to Kerala. With Ravi's help, he reached Palakkad, walking through the jungles and taking a bus now and then. Ravi's friend in Palakkad, one Mr Menon, provided him shelter for some time. Leon's men had cast a net for Jagan from Coonoor to Chennai. He grew a beard, wore Islamic clothes, and went around like a Muslim. Thus, he waited for his pursuers' enthusiasm to die down. Then, he came to Madurai via Dindigal. He was afraid to contact Olivia over the phone. He had an illusion that Leon's tentacles were spread everywhere. He calculated that they would surely observe Olivia also.

When Olivia had been searching for him, she had met his father's friend, Raghuraman Thanikachalam. She had also continued her contact with that family. They thought that Jagan had died. This time she had given him their phone number.

I am the Lord

When Jagan phoned, Raghuraman's wife took the call. On his introducing himself as Jagan, she disconnected the call. When he called again, she brought her husband. He too had believed that Jagan was dead. He assumed that the caller was a conman. Then, Jagan somehow convinced him to ask Olivia to contact them and talk to Jagan. The latter knew that Olivia was Jagan's friend. If he were a fraud, why should he name Olivia?

Finally, Raghuraman contacted Olivia. He invited her to his house, and helped her to talk to Jagan. The next day Olivia reached Madurai by train.

Should the reunion of lovers be described?

With great pride, Olivia said, "For the first time you have taken a decision and implemented it. All these years, others took decisions for you. I'm very happy and proud of this."

"I have brought only my passport, a little money, and a few dresses. I'm your beloved. If you are a MAN, you should protect yourself and me, and see that we reach Australia."

Olivia stopped talking and handed over the contact addresses and phone numbers given to her by Raghuraman.

"Why should you take risks for my sake? You go to Australia directly using your passport. I shall come there somehow and meet you," said Jagan, very practically.

"Just as you were the prisoner of religion, I'm the prisoner of love. How many years have I wasted, searching for you? I shall not leave you alone hereafter. Together we shall face any danger and emerge victorious."

During the next few days, Jagan drew up a plan. When Olivia was in Harvard University, she had worked for the New York Times, and had the ID of its reporter. As arranged by Raghuraman's friends, an ID of Dina Thanthi (a Tamil daily) and a letter of introduction for Jagan were prepared. Later, arrangements were made through the LTTE's agent near Rameswaram for the couple to go to Mannar, Sri Lanka, by boat. There, they were to function as reporters who had come to interview the LTTE leaders, and when they got a chance, to go to Colombo and surrender at the Australian Embassy there. This was their plan.

Taking a motorized boat, they crossed the Palk Straits in a few hours and reached the Vidathal Theevu near Mannar. From there they were taken to various LTTE camps. A vast difference exists, in the way the local and foreign journalists are treated. The ruling power intends that the local journalists should present only good news and hopes (of a bright future) to the people under its control. The local press has neither the strength nor the courage to function against the rulers' intention. Therefore, the local press remains

I am the Lord

supressed and its reporters are not given any importance.

The condition of the foreign press is different. Except for a few countries like North Korea whose borders are sealed, foreign journalists are received well in all other countries. This is because they want a rosy picture of their rule and its achievements to be presented, so that the world has a good opinion of their organisation and offers its support. At a time when the support of the Western world and India in particular was very necessary, it must have given them great happiness to see an American and an Indian journalist coming together simultaneously.

It was a time when the Sri Lankan army and the LTTE were strong in the Jaffna peninsula and the Vanni areas respectively. The Sri Lankan army was engaged in large-scale military activities in the Vanni region also, to control the Kandy road. This road cut the LTTE-controlled region into two. Even in the midst of all this military activity, the Tigers managed to cross from one side to the other quite easily.

The fauna and flora of Jaffna and the Vanni areas differed greatly from that of the rest of the country. Southern Sri Lanka abounded in coconut trees, whereas the North Eastern regions were full of palmyrahs. Not only the plant life, but the language and culture of the people were also different in the South and the North East.

The first sight that caught Jagan's attention on landing in the North was that of broken palmyrah trees! Several trees had been blown off by the shell attacks launched during the war. Many had been felled to strengthen the bunkers used to escape from the military attacks. The war had affected not only the plant life. As a young boy when Jagan had gone to Jaffna and Vanni for the vacation, he had seen and enjoyed the sight of various species of birds. Apart from the ubiquitous crows, cranes and storks, colourful birds like the shenbagam, yellow sparrows, cuckoos, different types of parrots, kingfishers, woodpeckers and so on used to frequent the place. Now, many of them had stopped coming there altogether, probably fearing the cruelties of war.

Roads, which had been crowded with men and vehicles, now looked deserted.

The two "journalists" were able to meet some of the second rung leaders. The latter explained why they had engaged themselves in this fight and what their goals were.

When the Europeans came to Sri Lanka, there were three kingdoms there. From the 16th to the 20th century, for nearly 400 years, Sri Lanka was in the hands of the Europeans. While the Tamil kingdom in the North and the Kotte kingdom in the South fell very early, the Kandyan kingdom alone retained its independence until 1815. The Portuguese and the Dutch were unable to capture the Kandyan kingdom. Although its citizens were mostly Sinhalese, its rulers were the descendants of the Madurai Nayakkars. Exploiting this difference and some of the atrocities inflicted by the king, the British brought the Kandyan kingdom also under their control, with the help of the Sinhalese chieftains, who turned against their ruler and betrayed the king.

The Sinhalese chieftains had betrayed the king, in the belief that the British would reclaim their kingdom from the Dravidian Nayakkars, and hand it over to them. Having captured the government, the British seized their lands from the people of Kandy, and set up large coffee and tea plantations there. To work in these plantations, the British brought in large numbers of workers from India, just as they had done in the Caribbean islands, South Africa and Fiji. Having brought the entire country under one rule, the British trained the locals for civil service in the government. The Tamils were mostly employed in the government jobs. There may have been various reasons for this. First, many missionary schools had been established in the Tamil areas. In arid lands (with scanty rainfall) like Jaffna, it was difficult to depend on cultivation and industries based on land resources. Hence, realizing that they could progress only through education, the Jaffna Tamils focused on learning. In addition, it is believed that the British followed the divide and rule policy, by which the aspirations of the majority could be controlled by using the minority. Due to these factors, compared to the size of their population, the number of Tamils in Government Service was disproportionately higher.

Sri Lanka attained independence without any struggle, bloodshed, or even sweat, unlike India. There had been no struggle for independence in Sri Lanka, such as the one in India. Sri Lanka's first Prime Minister won its freedom dressed like a British lord, with a tailcoat and top hat.

On the other hand, S.W.R.D.Bandaranaike, who grew up with a liking for all British things, gave up his English clothes for political gain and wore the national dress. He and the first Prime Minister D.S.Senanayake competed with each other to stoke nationalism. This consisted of acts that included the denial of citizenship to the plantation workers of Indian origin, making "Sinhala Only" the language of administration, and the settling of the Sinhalese in Tamil areas. Ethnic riots in which Sinhalese gangsters were allowed to run riot with the help of the police punctuated this. In the course of these riots, the Tamils' lives, possessions, chastity, and respect were all plundered.

The Tamils' fight for rights which began very peacefully, exploded into a large-scale war with India's support, after the 1983 ethnic riots. Subsequently, due to various incidents, the Tamils themselves fought against the Indian army, followed by the assassination of India's former Prime Minister, Rajiv Gandhi.

When Jagan and Olivia went there, the Sinhala army and the LTTE Tamils were locked in a serious conflict.

Because of the war, the Northern part of the island regressed to the Stone Age. With the acute shortage of electricity and fuel, transport was a big problem. The roads were full of potholes. Whenever a vehicle passed, there was a smell of fried eggs. This was how the people lived. Due to the lack of fuel for vehicles, a blend of vegetable oil and kerosene was used. Long before the Western countries started widespread use of vegetable oil as a renewable source of energy for vehicles, it was used in Northern Sri Lanka widely. But its contribution to environmental protection was nullified by the radiation and smoke emitted by the shells and the cutting of trees.

Jagan, who had lost some years of his life in the name of religion, could understand how in Sri Lanka Sinhalese nationalism and Buddhist religiosity combined to produce a Sinhalese Buddhist nationalism that ruined the island.

The Sinhalese, though a majority in Sri Lanka, are in a minority in the Indian sub-continent, and hence, in their fear tend to consider other minorities with suspicion. According to history, if a race feels that it has been wronged, and if an aggressive leader full of fury appears on the scene, the results can be disastrous. After World War I, it was the unjust peace imposed upon Germany, and the history-based suspicion and jealousy that the

Ezhuth Aani

others had for the Jews that produced a congenial atmosphere for the emergence of Hitler.

When Sri Lanka became independent, it acquired a sound economy and health service as a legacy. Due to the free education system introduced by C.W.W.Kannangara, the Sri Lankans were well educated, with a good understanding of politics. Hence, it was easy to generate rivalry and conflict between races. It makes one wonder sometimes, whether this was the gain of being educated!

Explaining this to Olivia, Jagan was proud to see the discipline and good conduct that he observed in the Tamil areas.

Olivia, on the other hand, asked him, "What is the difference between the discipline in this society and that in your Church?"

He had no answer to this. Whatever it may be, they agreed that the caste system that existed earlier was lesser now. Jagan, who in Colombo, had lived a life that paid no heed to caste distinctions, could not understand this difference.

'Silence is golden' says the proverb. If you violate this, you are in for trouble. Similarly, their journey, which had gone on smoothly so far, was spoilt by Jagan's talk. Yes, he asked for permission to interview the LTTE leader. That increased the scrutiny on them and the result landed as a thunderbolt on their heads.

I am the Lord

If one wished to interview the leader, he had to pass several safety barriers. Thus far, they had not been under the scrutiny of the Intelligence Agencies; but now, their antecedents were investigated in detail. Jagan spoke in the accent he had been used to, when he was in India. However, in the course of a long conversation, he could not help using the Jaffna slang.

Observing this closely, the investigating authorities began to eye him with suspicion.

Just as a frog betrays itself by its croaking, as Jagan continued talking, it became evident to the officers that he was not an Indian. What next? The mask was removed. Those who addressed him respectfully as 'brother' now regarded him as an infiltrator. The officers separated the lovers, and confined Olivia in a women's jail and Jagan in the men's prison. Though it was meant to be a prison, initially it appeared more like a hostel, where many like Jagan had been detained for interrogation. Compared to the 'torture' he had suffered under Gupta in India, this was much better, thought Jagan. In the name of an enquiry, for several hours every day, they kept asking him the same questions repeatedly. They compared his statements with the information given by Olivia, and asked him more questions.

There was nothing to hide. Knowing that there was no use hiding anything, Jagan confessed everything. Then, they questioned him with concern about the arms training given to him in

Afghanistan. They gave him some of the weapons they had, and asked him to demonstrate how to assemble and dismantle them, how to change the magazines and so on. By doing so, they compared what he had said with the skill he displayed, and checked whether he spoke the truth.

Every day, every one of them was interrogated by different groups or by individuals, and brought back to prison. As it was rumoured that there were spies inside the prison in the garb of prisoners, they were afraid even to talk to one another. On a few occasions, though Jagan and Olivia were interrogated together, she was taken to a women's prison elsewhere after the enquiry. At the end of all this, the authorities concluded that they were husband and wife.

One day, a gentleman was brought in. He was dressed in white. He was shown great respect there. With the familiar 'the Lord will save you' visiting card, he approached Jagan.

Yes. He was a Christian pastor. Had Jagan been his earlier self, this greeting would have given him great joy and hope. After his dialogues with Olivia, he had acquired sufficient maturity and self-confidence. Whether there was a God or not, the numerous obstacles he had crossed and overcome, gave him the strength to face, somehow or the other, any situation and challenge. This daring was a new experience for him.

I am the Lord

Though Jagan did not accept the gentleman's invitation, there were others who accepted his 'prize' called hope, with both their hands.

The relationship that exists between the neo-Christians and the Liberation Movements is a symbiotic one. That is, the Liberation Movements must have gained something from the former. At the same time, they offered a kind of solace to the suppressed. There are many who argue that Jesus Christ was the world's first Communist. Similarly, in South America, the so-called Liberation Theology dawned in the 1950s. That was the time when Fidel Castro came to power, and revolutionaries like Che Guevara built revolutionary movements in South America and brought about a Renaissance in the Communist Movement. But the Vatican declared them as anti-Christian in the 80s, and ostracized them. There is a world of difference between the religious movements with Communist leanings, and the neo-Christianism exported by America and the Western countries. In conformity with Christ's doctrine 'Give unto Caesar what belongs to him' and Paul's dictum that one should accommodate those in power, the latter functioned in their respective spheres without challenging the rulers who wielded authority.

Many parts of the Bible, especially the Old Testament, mirrored the loss and tragedy of the people during times of war, and later promised them a bright and prosperous future. It is no wonder therefore, that these words written for the

Jews scattered by the conquerors offer a consolation to the suppressed wherever they are, whoever they may be.

Organizations like the Liberation Tigers obtained certain benefits from these Churches. Having banned the means of entertainment such as films and film music, and having fed the people with news only of war and sorrow, they allowed such religious organizations in their areas, to channelize the people's frustration, before it developed into dissatisfaction with and opposition against their activities. At the same time, they did not encourage Movements like Hare Rama and Sai Baba, which functioned with India as their inspiration. It may have been because they always looked upon India with suspicion.

At the same time, they were apprehensive of suppressing Churches that had the support of Western countries – both financially and media-wise. They knew that if they had to establish their independence surpassing the regional supremacy of India diplomatically, they needed the West's friendship and goodwill. Hence, they hesitated in indulging in any act that would project them as religiously intolerant.

When they realised they were from Australia, on this basis, that they did not harm Olivia and her dependant Jagan. Initially, though they beat him up a little, later they treated him quite decently.

I am the Lord

As soon as they realized that Jagan knew Sinhalese fluently, they engaged in trying to convert him to their way of thinking. They repeatedly told him how the Tamils were side-lined in higher education and jobs, and how the Sri Lankan as well as the Indian armies committed atrocities in the North East.

They told him that suicide bombing was a poor man's weapon. Their argument was that this was the only weapon, which could be used against an enemy who had the backing of the money and military might of many imperialist countries. They claimed that these suicide bombers or their families had been directly affected by violence unleashed by the oppressor.

The present Jagan was different from his earlier self. He was not the Jagan who formerly involved himself in others' struggles and injustices easily, and identified himself with them.

As their propaganda continued, Jagan took a few resolutions deep down in his mind. First, he would not be a party to violence. Second, he now had the responsibility of protecting Olivia. Third, somehow they should leave that place. With his present maturity, he understood all this very clearly. A majority of the people in his life were trying to exploit him in some way. They were affectionate towards him only with a specific agenda. Unconditional love was rare in reality.

In life, some are educated and employed. Others run an organization and earn their livelihood. These organizations may be religious, political, or service-oriented.

Even in international service organizations, more than 50 per cent of the donations that they collect are spent on the maintenance of their employees and on infrastructure.

Thus, their life went on, with enquiries and propaganda being the daily routine. He accustomed himself to this also. At the same time, he refused to submit to their ways. He was not inclined to reveal his innermost secrets openly.

About this time, a crowd had begun to gather around that preacher. Jagan doubted whether he was a real preacher or a spy sent by his captors. This was because, many of the prisoners, in the name of a confession, had begun to own their misdeeds. However, Jagan maintained a respectful distance from him. He was not prepared to be caught in that hamster wheel again.

Two months had passed thus in the prison, when one day, two men whom he had not met before, came and spoke to him in a very friendly manner. For the next two or three days, Jagan and Olivia were treated royally. They were allowed to stay together.

The reason for this change was revealed to them on the second day itself. To find out whether

I am the Lord

what they had said was true, the captors had approached their international agents who confirmed that what they had said was true. Moreover, Raghuraman had pressurized the authorities through his friends to allow Jagan to return safely. Apart from this, there was another reason also. It was not revealed to him.

The newcomers behaved very caringly and decently to Jagan and Olivia. They said that the couple would be released during the next few days, and that they were only waiting for the order to come from their leader.

They were informed that a Red Cross van would take them to Colombo, and after that, it was their responsibility to get in touch with the Australian Embassy.

Subsequently, they were given permission to go about 'freely'. This was a new connotation of the word 'freedom'. On one side was a cruel enemy; on the other, the guerrilla army that opposed him; in between, where could they roam about freely? Compared to their prison life, this appeared to be heavenly, for Jagan.

Even in the gruesomeness of the war, Mother Nature had not lost her beauty. The dense forests of Vanni dotted by springs provided an ideal backdrop for Sunrise and Sunset. The broken palms lay beside the tall ones that were still standing. If only the war had not taken place, the whole world would have come to see this bounty of Nature.

It was their last day in Vanni. They had been advised, "Be ready to leave early tomorrow morning." That evening, they sat under a tree by a pond, watching the sunset.

Jagan asked, "Why are they releasing us?"

"Our people must have pressurized them. That is one reason. But there should certainly be another one" replied Olivia.

"Nothing is available for free in this world. Even for something that you think you got freely, you will have to pay indirectly," she cautioned, pouting her lips.

"Really? In that case, what price do the winners pay for the huge amounts they get in a lottery?" asked Jagan with a smile.

"A lottery prize is like a loan that you take from your Karma. Some day you will have to pay a price for it," said Olivia. Both of them knew several stories of husband and wife separating, due to quarrels resulting from the winning of a lottery suddenly.

"Then what was your expectation in reclaiming me from my illusion?" asked Jagan.

I am the Lord

She could not answer that. "Yes. In life, sometimes some people receive love from others who do not expect anything in return. We cannot reason them out."

"What do you think of religions?" asked Jagan.

"Spirituality is one thing. Religion is another. Religions are like a franchise – a chain of sales outlets. If you want to eat chicken, you can do so in Macdonald's, KFC, or Burgher King. Or you can cook it at home also and eat. Religions are symbols of culture and they have nothing to do with spirituality," said Olivia.

She then took a stone and threw it into the pond. Ripples spread from the point where it fell, in all directions in circles. Shortly, the pond looked serene and smooth again. She said, "Ripples appear and disappear only on the surface of the mind. Deep down the mind is pacific. You do not know its depth. If you probe and understand the sub-conscious, you will realize that the sorrows and disturbances that appear and disappear in life, will not affect the sub-conscious."

"What do you think of idol worship?"

"Strike this tree and see! How solid it is! What is it made of? Atoms. You know that 95 per cent of an atom is empty space! Yes, a space in which electrons roam about. You consider this tree, made up of atoms, the major part of which is vacant space, as a solid object. Accept that this is an

Ezhuth Aani

illusion. This Universe itself is made up of space and vibrations. Hence, even a stone idol, when worshipped with single-minded devotion, can increase its vibrations, is it not? How can you then say that it is only a stone statue?"

"From ancient times, many have threatened us saying that the world was going to end. You must have heard of Nostradamus' prophecy. In recent times, Jehovah's Witnesses predicted the end of the world on different dates, and later, when it did not eventuate, postponed it to another date. Similarly, the founder of the Calvary Chapel, Chuck Smith, predicted the end of the world on certain dates, but nothing happened. What is ironical about this whole thing is the fact, that though none of these prophecies came true, the people belonging to the various Churches do not question their leaders, and are in fact, quite willing to trust them!"

"Like some species of moths that are attracted by fire fall in it and die, these people waste their lives."

"Have you seen how your Tamil poet Bharathi handled this example of the fire? That is, 'the fire that you lit in your mind should burn the forest of ignorance in this world. But you should not fall into it'".

Sometimes, we respect our culture and traditions only when they come to us through foreigners. Likewise, the great poet Bharathi who

I am the Lord

mesmerized people with his Tamil is brought to Jagan only through Olivia.

As they were talking thus, Jagan tried to hug Olivia. Refusing to accede with an 'Hmm', Olivia said politely, "This is not Vellaiyangiri hills. Here, even trees have eyes! Hence, restrain yourself until we go back to our room."

Later, they went to their allotted place, had dinner, and in the embrace of 'sleep' travelled to another world.

Refreshed after a good night's sleep, they woke up at dawn, to the sounds of the birds and the rustle of the leaves disturbed by the slight drizzle of rain, with the lush green carpet of grass bathed in the blood-red sunlight. The thought that they would be freed that day, excited and delighted them. The sound of the shells heard daily at a distance, was not heard that day.

They were asked to come for breakfast. Another gentleman was seated there. "His name is Amalan. He will accompany you to Colombo," said the commander of the camp.

Through the Australian Embassy, temporary transit documents had been arranged for Jagan. Olivia's passport was returned to her. They were taken by a Red Cross van. Both of them sat in front, while Amalan sat at the back. He did not talk much. Though not eager to converse, he observed all the goings-on very carefully.

Ezhuth Aani

The driver's name was Parthan. He was a Red Cross employee. He had the experience of having travelled to Colombo often. He spoke to Olivia in the broken English, which he knew.

Olivia was dressed in a churidar like an Indian woman. It enhanced her beauty further. In truth, the churidar was a North Indian dress. Just as men had discarded their traditional dresses and begun to wear trousers and shirts, South Indian and Sri Lankan women including the Sinhalese, had adopted the churidar as their national dress.

This was a great victory for North Indian culture, won without arms, bloodshed, and the imposition of a language. Now, a foreigner too, was wearing it.

Their belongings had been packed and loaded into the vehicle.

Though everything was ready, Parthan hesitated, as if expecting something. When asked why, he replied that the leave permit had not been obtained. Those who do not have it cannot move out of the area under the guerrillas' control.

Having waited for nearly an hour, they were tired. In the lives of the North Eastern people, where shortages and control were quite common, an hour's delay was not unusual. Jagan had been accustomed to such delays during his stay in Afghanistan. Olivia was restless to leave.

I am the Lord

It was then, that the commander came running in a hurry. He took Jagan separately to his office.

"We've got your pass. But we need a personal favour from you" he said.

"What favour?"

"In addition to your baggage, I will give you another small parcel. My friend will receive it from you in Colombo."

"That depends on what is in the parcel," said Jagan.

All this while, the commander had been speaking patiently and in a friendly manner; but now his face darkened. He looked at Jagan severely and said, "Your pass will be valid only if you obtain permission from another department. It is on my personal surety that we are allowing you to go today. For that, you should do as I say. Otherwise you cannot go today."

Realizing that once again they were being exploited, Jagan's heartbeats went haywire.

Just then, Olivia too came there, and both of them spoke in English. Though the commander understood what they were talking about, he remained silent with his hands folded across his chest. Around forty years of age, he was nearly six feet tall. He had a huge moustache and several scars on his face. His face was light brown, but the scars that were lighter gave him a very stern appearance. Though he presented a calm exterior, it was clear that he would not change his mind.

Jagan was angry at the calm but firm tone in which he spoke sparingly, but he also felt a kind of respect towards him. After reflecting for a while, he agreed to his condition.

Having somehow overcome all the obstacles, their journey began.

Due to military activities, the roads were full of potholes and stones. In many places, it was slushy, and in some places, the water stagnated in small pools. They had been advised not to go to the sides of the road. It was feared that land mines might have been planted on the sides. Hence, as the vehicle went up and down the bumpy road, their backs, and hips began to ache. Somehow, they crossed Vavuniya. As the government authorities had been informed in advance about their arrival, there was not much of a scrutiny.

# 3

Amalan did not speak anything. From the backseat, he observed their talk and behavior intently. As they approached Anuradhapura city, Parthan stopped at an eatery. Jagan and Olivia sat at a table, while Amalan sat at an adjacent table and kept a watch on them as he ate. Then Jagan wrote something on the table in Greek. 'We should escape at an opportune moment' was his message. As Olivia's parents spoke Greek, he had picked up a little of the language on his visits to their house. Moreover, as Olivia's brothers were his friends, he was used to talking to them in their language. Though the Greek letters were different from the English ones, one could use Roman letters to write Greek words. Although Amalan noticed them writing on the table, since he could not understand what it was, he assumed that it was the usual lovers' nonsensical chat.

Anuradhapura was not only Sri Lanka's ancient capital, but also the place where the Duttagemunu-Elara story had been played out. It was also the arena of the competition between the great Buddhist monasteries of Mahavihara, Abhayagiri, and Jetthavanarama. Although initially, Abhayagiri, which followed the Mahayana tradition, won, the Mahavihara Theros who followed Theravada Buddhism enthroned Theravada in the name of religious integration during the reign of King Parakramabahu the Great.

Ezhuth Aani

Mahanama Thero was one of the Mahavihara high priests. It was the book *Mahavamsa*, written by Mahanama Thero, which several centuries later sowed the seed for the growth of the politics combined Sinhalese-Buddhist nationalism. Yes. Need there be another example for the saying, 'The pen is mightier than the Sword?'

As soon as they left Anuradhapura, they had an illusory feeling of entering a new world. Yes! During times of war, Anuradhapura functioned as the frontier town of the Sinhalese. The military and air force camps, and the hospital had been strengthened and reinforced manifold, and they served as the rear bases for the armed forces.

Once they passed Anuradhapura, the country looked more or less normal. Since the skirmishes of war took place in the North East, the majority of the Sinhalese did not have to encounter the ugly face of war, except for sporadic bombings. Hence, all forms of entertainment from cricket to music and dance went on there as usual.

Moreover, the lusciousness and abundance found in the rain-rich Southern Sri Lanka were certainly more than those of the dry North. Just as the North was full of palmyrahs, the South had coconut trees in plenty.

The army and police checkpoints that dotted the near-normal Southern Sri Lanka, reminded one of the fact that the war had not ended.

I am the Lord

Their vehicle had crossed Anuradhapura and was heading towards Puttalam. With rows of coconut trees and clusters of long reeds lining both sides of the road, the van was going faster than before. Jagan and Olivia were waiting for the right opportunity. They realized that somehow, before reaching Colombo they had to escape from the vehicle and from Amalan's custody. If they reached Colombo in Amalan's company, his friends would join him. After that how they would be exploited, was a disturbing question. Whatever be the case, Jagan was determined not to abet violence of any kind.

When the van reached Negombo, Parthan stopped again to have tea. Olivia wanted to use the toilet, which was separate from the tea kiosk, and located in the adjacent basement. While the men eased themselves under the trees, the women used only that toilet. Sometimes they had to wait in a queue for this.

As there were many women waiting, Amalan did not accompany them. He waited for them in the shop. After they had gone a little distance, Jagan said 'now'. Immediately, he held Olivia's hand and ran between the coconut trees towards the seashore. Both of them ran hiding in between the trees on the beach.

In the distance, Amalan could be seen running towards them. He had a gun in his hand. He did not attempt to shoot them; because, he knew that if the others heard the gunshot, their attention would be drawn towards them and the important bundle that was in the vehicle would be seized. At the same time, he was scared that if they escaped they might inform the police. Hence, his aim was to threaten them with the gun and force them into the van.

On one side, the sea waves rolled back and forth on the white sand. On the other, Amalan was approaching them with a gun. A decision had to be taken now. If they ran, he might shoot. If he shot, more than what would happen to him, Jagan was apprehensive that anything could happen to Olivia.

He spoke to Amalan. "If you shoot us, your plot will be exposed. Allow us to go on our way." Without replying, Amalan was engrossed in approaching Jagan.

Jagan stood with his hands raised, until Amalan came close to him, and shouting 'Run' to Olivia, he pounced upon Amalan. Before Amalan could recover from a second's hesitation, Jagan bent his wrist and seized his gun.

Amalan was shocked by this sudden turn of events. Jagan shouted to him: "Keep your hands behind and walk back."

As Amalan hesitated little, Jagan said, "Don't think I do not know to shoot. I have had military training in Afghanistan."

I am the Lord

"I can shoot you if needed. But I don't like unnecessary loss of life. However, if you don't do as I tell you, I'll shoot you mercilessly." Jagan's determination was evident in his voice.

Amalan had no choice except to obey Jagan. As soon as he was out of sight, Jagan asked Olivia to run with him along the seashore.

Jagan knew Negombo very well. In his childhood, he had come several times to Negombo with his family. Walking and running in turn, they reached the railway station at Negombo. If they went along the tracks, they could get into the train without any tickets. He had seen others do this. Since they did not have any Sri Lankan currency, he too did the same now.

As he could speak Sinhalese fluently, he did not have any problem in the train. As he was with her, nobody questioned Olivia.

Their passports and other travel documents were in the van itself. Somehow, if they reached the Australian Embassy they believed that the officials there would help them. She broke the silence that prevailed.

"Your Valluvar says, 'How much ever you learn it will not equal the real knowledge within you'. Whether you learn the Bhagavad Gita, the Bible, or the Quran, it will not be equal to the humanitarianism, sympathy and love which are within you, that is, within every human being."

Ezhuth Aani

"I see some changes in you. Earlier, you could be shaped by anybody;
i.e., for every little thing you depended on others for advice and direction. You were not able to take a decision for yourself and implement it with resolve. But once you released yourself from Leon's control, you have been able to take decisions independently and carry them out. I like it very much," said Olivia emotionally and happily.

"All because of you," said Jagan.

"How's that?" asked Olivia.

"From the day we were united, I had the responsibility of taking care not only of myself but also you," said Jagan.

"Don't cite me as the reason. Everything is within you. When you realize yourself, your body, mind and actions are all focused. Hence, you become the agent of your achievements as well as your failures. Know that."

Just then, two army men entered the compartment. They had machine guns with them. But they were not pointed towards the people. An army man, who appeared as a stranger, an intruder, and an aggressor in the North Eastern regions, was looked upon here as a friend or a brother. It was reflected in the manner in which he behaved among the people.

I am the Lord

He examined whether the passengers had an identity card. If those who did not have one spoke Sinhalese fluently, he left them without any harassment. Noticing this, Jagan began conversing with him of his own accord. Their dialogue, which began with the introductory words, *'Raalahaami Kohomatha'*, continued on a casual note. He told the army man that he was working in the Katunayaka Free Trade Zone and that his wife belonged to Australia. Their conversation, which consisted of short tit bits such as 'Will it rain today?' ended with the army man's tribute to Olivia's beauty, *'Maathayage powla hari lassana'*. He did not ask for their ID cards.\

After he left, Olivia asked, "Why did you not shoot Amalan?"

He replied, "Human life is invaluable. Although the Gita says that one can kill even a cow in self-defence, I do not believe in unnecessary violence."

"What did you do with the gun then?" asked Olivia.

"It has reached the depths of the Negombo Sea. Nobody can find it for the time being."

"Why didn't you tell the police about Amalan?" asked Olivia again.

"As an individual, I shall never abet violence. In the battle between two violent groups, I am not prepared to betray any one of them. Both believe that they are fighting for justice. Who am I to pronounce a judgment?" asked Jagan.

"One of the warring groups belongs to your race. Your own flesh and blood. In spite of that, why didn't you think of supporting it?" asked Olivia.

"First and foremost, I am an Australian. My first duty is towards my country. Second, I am your lover or husband. My second duty is to protect and keep you happy. I do not want to go beyond this and join them. Another point; only now I have succeeded in extricating myself from being exploited by others. I am not prepared to return to that predicament again."

As soon as he said this, Olivia hugged and kissed him.

"Be careful! Kissing in public has not become common here," said Jagan.

He then knelt and asked her, "Will you marry me?"

"Certainly" said Olivia. "But I'll always be a Christian. You should always be a Hindu. Do you agree to that?"

"After my experiences in life, I have realized that religious conversion is a baseless, retrogressive philosophy. As Kannadasan said, if

I am the Lord

everyone remains in his place, everyone will be well and happy. When a man changes his religion, he cuts his roots. Even a hybrid mango fruit retains its quality and taste, though it is rootless. But a man without roots is neither here nor there, and lives in a 'midway' hell."

"If there are several forms of treatment for a disease, what we should understand is the fact, that none of those forms is better than the others. If it were so, the other forms of treatment will fall into disuse, and in course of time decay and die. The same with religions also. If any religion were to be superior to the others, all the people would follow that religion. No religion has been found to be better than the others. If there were a true or perfect religion, there would be no need for a knife or gun to propagate it. Moreover, there is no need to use a false threat 'Destruction is on the way', to frighten people. Religions are only the water used to satisfy man's spiritual thirst, nothing more. The water can be in the form of orange juice, or apple juice, or even grape juice. Or it can be just pure water. What the body needs is water. The others are merely for the tongue's taste.

"When a train runs on its track, it travels safely, with a kind of rhythm and sound. When it tries to change tracks, the chances of derailment increase.

"When a man changes his religion, he turns his back not only on his childhood, parents, and relatives. He turns his back on his forefathers, heredity, and all his traditional values. He may float in the dream that he can go to heaven. Did all his ancestors sleeping in their graves or their ashes go to hell?

"If a man were to regard another as his brother or as an equal, he will never ask him to change his religion. Because we consider him inferior to us, we ask him to convert.

"If everyone in this world realizes this truth, the world would turn into heaven. But ... some people will lose their livelihood... Yes; they will be compelled to find other means of employment to survive!"

The train was nearing Colombo ...

### ***THE END***

I am the Lord

# Revolution

Pristine were the snow caps

The rain and the icicles

Pure and white in intent

The river flows from the high lands

The freshness is life giving

As it journeys through the countryside

It acquires the characters of the soil And the people

It takes the redness, the richness

It smells of the flowers, the trees

The roots that protrude and filter

The fruits that enrich The grass that grow by

The beautiful countryside

The lakes, the waterfalls, the rocks

The romantic odour

A majestic march indeed

The pride of the nation

The cradle of civilization

Then it reaches its destination –

The enforced uniformity

The salinity
The conformity....

What has become of thou?

Ezhuth Aani

www.ingramcontent.com/pod-product-compliance
Lightning Source LLC
Chambersburg PA
CBHW021234250626
47155CB00008B/3008